Frank _____ l,
but pu _____ g
darkne _____ n
feet fr _____ y
fingers

Joe pu _____ k
could _____ ff
his fin

"We n _____ e
rested _____ "
Frank _____ s
the re

Witho _____ o
time t _____ d
into th

The Hardy Boys Mystery Stories

Available from MINSTREL Books

THE HARDY BOYS®

141

THE DESERT THIEVES

FRANKLIN W. DIXON

A MINSTREL® BOOK

Published by POCKET BOOKS
New York London Toronto Sydney Tokyo Singapore

This book is a work of fiction. Names, characters, places and incidents are products of the author's imagination or are used fictitiously. Any resemblance to actual events or locales or persons, living or dead, is entirely coincidental.

A MINSTREL PAPERBACK *Original*

A Minstrel Book published by
POCKET BOOKS, a division of Simon & Schuster Inc.
1230 Avenue of the Americas, New York, NY 10020

Copyright © 1996 by Simon & Schuster Inc.

Front cover illustration by Lee MacLeod

Produced by Mega-Books, Inc.

ISBN: 0-671-50527-0

First Minstrel Books printing December 1996

10   9   8   7   6   5   4   3   2   1

THE HARDY BOYS MYSTERY STORIES is a trademark of Simon & Schuster Inc.

THE HARDY BOYS, A MINSTREL BOOK and colophon are registered trademarks of Simon & Schuster Inc.

Printed in the U.S.A.

Contents

1 A Near Miss

"I thought the desert would be nothing but sand dunes," Joe Hardy said. "There isn't any sand here, let alone dunes."

Standing beside a white U.S. Forest Service car, Joe looked out at a sweep of pale green trees, dark green bushes, and cacti growing from sand-colored earth. A hundred yards away, a mountain with rocky cliffs rose steeply out of the desert. In the distance were other brown hills and mountains.

Joe thought it felt strange to be wearing just a T-shirt and jeans in the dead of winter, but he was having no trouble getting used to it. He and his older brother, Frank, were on winter break from school. Fenton Hardy, their father, had brought them with him on a business trip to Arizona. Once Fenton had completed his business, they'd rented a

1

motor home and driven two hundred miles into the desert for a surprise visit to Winton Grisham, an old college friend of Fenton's.

Joe leaned against the car and looked over at his father and Frank, who, like him, were wearing sunglasses. His father was catching up on things with Grisham, or Grish, as he liked to be called. What a cool job, Joe thought, to be a park ranger at Organ Pipe Cactus National Monument. It was the largest natural preserve in the lower forty-eight states, right on the U.S.–Mexico border. Joe thought Grisham looked every inch the part of head park ranger. A burly man with sandy hair and large, powerful hands, he wore a cowboy hat and a green shirt with a name tag.

To make the trip more interesting, though, Joe almost wished they could find some sort of mystery to solve. Back in their hometown of Bayport, Frank and Joe spent much of their time investigating crimes and had become crack detectives, even though Joe was only seventeen and his brother eighteen. Their father was a famous professional detective, and the brothers had learned a lot from him.

Grish tipped his hat back and reached into the trunk of his car for a large water jug and some cups. He poured four cups of water and handed three of them to the Hardys.

"This is typical weather for early January," Grish said in answer to Frank's question. "The daytime temperatures are in the fifties or sixties. Summer-

2

time highs are well above a hundred, though, which is why we have a rule about always carrying water."

"The plants here don't seem to need much water," Frank said. "They look tough."

Joe pointed to a small cactus. "Those spines look like something I wouldn't want to tangle with," Joe said.

Grish smiled. "That cactus is called a jumping cholla. Pieces of it can break off and stick to your foot or hand so easily they seem to jump right off the plant. Out on the range, you can sometimes see cattle with pieces of cholla stuck to their lips."

"Yikes," Joe said, stepping away from the cactus.

"As I was saying, the rains are often months apart," Grish said. "To conserve water, the cacti swell up and store it in their tissues."

Pointing to a tall, slender cactus that looked like a rocket ship with arms, Joe asked Grisham what it was.

"That's a saguaro cactus. It's the one that a lot of people think of when they think about the desert here in the Southwest."

Then he pointed to another cactus in the distance. "See that tall one over there?" About fifteen feet tall, it looked like a cluster of many long, tubular branches that started at the ground and came up to a rounded tip. "It's called an organ pipe cactus. This park is named for them—Organ Pipe Cactus National Monument. All the wildlife and plants here are protected. To disturb or remove anything is considered a violation."

3

Grisham glanced at his watch. "But listen, I have to get you guys back to the campground. I've got some work to do at my office before suppertime."

"Right, and we should start fixing some grub," Frank said. "Isn't that how they say it out here in the West?"

"Well, not anymore," Grish said, shaking his head with amusement. "Maybe they used to."

"Grish, how about joining us for dinner at the campground?" Fenton asked. "We've got a lot of catching up to do after all these years."

Grish said, "That would be great, but I have to get a few things done first. Say, how long has it been since we've seen each other?"

"About twenty years, old friend," Fenton said.

Grish got into the car on the driver's side and said, "I hate to think it's been that long."

The three Hardys climbed in, with Frank and Joe in back. As Grish drove, Joe ran a hand through his blond hair and looked at the thick vegetation. He wondered how any living thing could survive the heat and dryness of summer.

As if to answer his question, Grish said, "This desert probably looks pretty harsh to you boys. In fact, during the day, when the heat is most intense, most of the creatures keep themselves sheltered. At night, though, they all come out looking for food."

"How do they find food in the dark?" Joe asked.

"Good noses and good night vision," Grish said. "Some eat seeds and leaves, and others go hunting

4

for the ones that eat seeds and leaves. You'll hear the coyotes tonight for certain. They sing all night."

Grish drove along a one-way dirt road that wound around the mountain.

"Those cliffs look pretty steep," Frank said. "With all the tourists around, do you ever have a problem with climbers getting hurt?" The Hardys were trained rock climbers. They had brought along ropes and gear, hoping to do some climbing in this strange environment.

"There are accidents every year," Grish said. "You can count on that. Those little mountains beside us are called the Diablos—the Devil Mountains. In the winter we usually have to rescue a few people who don't know how to climb safely. No problem with climbers in the summer, though: the rocks are too hot to touch, and nobody with any sense goes climbing."

At that moment something odd at the side of the road caught Joe's eye. He looked out the window and saw bushes crushed flat, as if someone had driven a truck over them.

"Whoa!" Joe exclaimed. "Grish, stop! Look back there. Someone's been doing some serious off-road driving."

The car skidded to a stop. "Where?" Fenton asked.

"Right back there," Joe said. "Grish, back up a bit."

Grish backed the car along the road until they drew even with the path of crushed plants. Parallel tracks from a heavy vehicle ran for two dozen yards. Perpendicular to the road, they were marked by crushed and broken branches. Two yards past the end of the tracks was a hole about four feet across, as far as Joe could tell. He could also make out several small crushed pulpy cacti that had been destroyed by the careless driver and were now bleeding a white liquid.

"What in the world happened here?" Fenton asked. "This is a disaster."

Grish said nothing for a moment, then drew a long breath. "It's a disaster, all right," he said. "This national park is a protected area. Someone is clearly defacing this land. We've got a situation here that needs to be dealt with."

"Who would do something like this?" Joe asked. "Off-roaders?" He began to open his door to get out, but Grish stopped him.

"We don't have time to stop right now, Joe," Grish said. "I've already seen the damage." He put the car into gear and pulled away.

"Those aren't the tracks of an off-road vehicle," Frank said. "See the double-tire marks? Those must have been made by a large truck."

"What's the story, Grish?" Fenton asked.

Grish said, "Those tracks were found this morning. I wasn't going to say anything, because I'm a stickler for the rules, and the rules say I'm not supposed to discuss an ongoing investigation."

"But who would drive a big truck out in the desert?" Frank asked.

6

"Cactus thieves," Grish said.

Frank and Joe responded in unison: "Cactus thieves?"

"Yes," Grish said. "Cactus thieves. Someone has been stealing large cactus specimens—saguaros and organ pipes mostly, as far as I can tell. I'm pretty sure I know who is involved. It's one of my maintenance workers, David Kidwell. I think I'll be having him arrested pretty soon."

"What makes you think it's him?" Frank asked. "How many maintenance workers do you have?"

"I have three others," Grish said, "but Kidwell used to be a landscaper in Phoenix, working with a nursery specializing in desert plants. He's the only one who would know how to remove large specimens."

Joe pointed toward an organ pipe cactus and said, "Those long arms look as if they would break off if someone tried to move the plant."

Grish nodded. "That is true of a large plant like that one, yes. But a medium-size one could have its arms braced with ropes and a wooden frame. Even a large organ pipe could be stolen if the thieves knew what they were doing."

"Why would anyone want to steal a cactus?" Frank asked.

"Money," Grish told him. "Desert landscaping is becoming popular in the cities of the Southwest. People like to plant cactus and other desert flora in their yards. Builders get more money from newcomers if the development looks like the desert.

Some of them will pay lots of money for good specimens of rare types. Of course, organ pipe cacti must be planted where there is no frost, but there are areas of California and Texas like that. A large, professionally transplanted organ pipe specimen would be worth thousands of dollars."

"Wow!" Joe said. "I had no idea."

"Isn't it a federal offense to disturb the desert habitat?" Fenton said.

"Absolutely," Grish said. "The term we use for stealing cacti is cactus rustling. Just like the cattle rustling from the days of the Old West."

"How many cacti have you lost?" Frank asked.

"I'm not sure," Grish said. "Ten or twelve, maybe. Right now I'm hoping to catch Kidwell in the act. But I'd appreciate it if you guys would let the matter drop and not talk about it. The investigation has been going on for a couple of months, and you're only here for a few days. I don't want the thieves to get spooked by too much talk. And besides, it's the rule."

"I think you know you can trust us," Fenton said to Grisham.

"Maybe Joe and I can help you with the investigation," Frank volunteered.

Grish looked skeptical. "No offense," he said, "but I doubt that a couple of amateur detectives tramping all over the desert would be much help."

An indignant look flashed across Joe's face. "Amateur?" he repeated.

"It's okay, Joe," Frank said. "Chill out. Maybe

8

we'll just keep our eyes open while we're on vacation here."

"Well, as I said," Grish replied, "no offense, but this is a job for someone who knows the territory. I've even asked for help from a cactus cop in Phoenix. The problem is that government budgets are being cut, people are being laid off, and it takes longer to get things done. I'm pretty frustrated with the whole system."

"A cactus cop?" Fenton asked.

"I'm not kidding," Grish said. "Arizona has investigators called cactus cops who try to stop the cactus rustlers."

Joe laughed. "That sounds a lot like the marshal going after the cattle rustlers," he said. "We really are in the Old West, aren't we?"

"Well, not exactly the *Old* West," Grish said. "But some things don't change much."

Joe pointed ahead toward a plume of dust rising above the desert along the road. "Look at that dust trail," he said. "Someone is headed this way pretty fast."

"Sometimes the tourists go tearing along these roads as if they were racing in the Indy Five Hundred," Grish said. "It makes me mad."

"I think you're forgetting something," Frank said, growing tense. "This is a one-way road. Whoever that is is headed right at us."

Grish's eyes grew wide. "You're right!" he exclaimed. A small blue pickup truck had come around the bend and was barreling straight at them.

9

2 The Trouble with Big Ears

Grish veered sharply to the edge of the road, barely in time to avoid a head-on collision. The blue pickup roared past, leaving the air thick with dust.

"Who was that?" Joe cried. "We could have been killed!"

Grish set his jaw with determination, wheeled the car around, and took off into the dust after the blue pickup. "That was David Kidwell," Grish said tightly. "I don't know what he's up to this time, but he can't go around forcing people off the road."

Grish's fingers gripped the wheel angrily as he squinted through the windshield, straining to see beyond the thick dust cloud being thrown up by the other vehicle. Joe and Frank tried to catch a glimpse of the pickup, but it had too much of a head start. Gradually the dust cleared, but by then the blue truck was gone from view.

"If I remember right," Frank said, "there aren't any turnoffs along this road. Unless he heads across the desert, we should catch up with him."

"The problem is that all the roads in this park are a one-way loop," Grish explained. "It cuts down on damage to the desert and accidents way out here. He's going the wrong way, and he's going so fast he could have a head-on with another vehicle."

At that moment they spotted the blue pickup ahead, stopped at the side of the road. When they drew nearer, they saw that it was parked at the site of the destruction they had seen earlier. A tall man with dark hair was walking toward the truck with a shovel in his hand. He wore a gray work uniform and appeared to be about twenty-five. He scowled as Grish pulled up behind the pickup.

Grish leaped from the car and slammed his door as Frank, Joe, and Fenton also climbed out.

"What do you think you're doing, Kidwell?" Grish yelled. "Are you crazy? You know as well as I do that this is a one-way road."

Kidwell stood unmoving, shovel in hand. "I came to get my shovel," he said.

"Your shovel?" Grish asked, incredulously. "Your *shovel?* You almost ran us off the road driving like a madman—for a *shovel?*"

Kidwell nodded. "That's it," he said. "It was my dad's shovel. I was afraid it would be gone by the time I got here."

11

"Why would you be afraid of that?" Frank asked.

Kidwell looked Frank up and down, seeming to be aware of the Hardys for the first time. "Who are you?" he said to Frank.

"I'm Frank Hardy. This is my brother, Joe, and our father, Fenton. I was just wondering why you would be afraid your shovel would be missing from a place like this, out in the middle of nowhere."

Kidwell shrugged. "I'm not supposed to talk about it," he said.

"Not supposed to talk about what?" Joe asked.

Kidwell looked at Grish, then said, "Nothing. Forget it. Sorry I scared you." He laid the shovel in the back of his truck, opened the cab door, and got in. "I gotta go. Guess you'll want to talk to me in the morning, boss?"

"You guessed right," Grish said with a touch of sarcasm. "First thing. Be on time."

"No problem," Kidwell said. He started his truck, turned sharply across the roadway, and then headed out in the correct direction along the one-way road.

"What was that all about, Grish?" Frank asked. "He's not the most talkative guy in the world, is he?"

Grish opened his door and motioned for the Hardys to get in. "You're right," he said. "Kidwell doesn't say much. But I've given him and the other maintenance people explicit instructions that if they discuss the investigation, they'll be put on administrative leave."

12

"You mean they'll be fired?" Joe asked, as Grish turned the car around and headed back toward the campground.

"More like they'll be suspended for a while without pay," Grish said.

"I don't understand," Frank said. "You said you don't want a lot of talk about the investigation to spook the thieves. And you suspect that Kidwell is one of the thieves. But he knows about the investigation?"

"That's right," Grish said. "I can't hide the fact that an investigation is under way. All my workers know about it, and so do some of the long-term residents of the campground. As for the details of the investigation, though, that's another matter."

"How long has Kidwell been working for you?" Frank asked.

"About two months," Grish said. "He knows a lot about the ecosystem here. He's quiet and seems to be a very thorough worker. I thought he was going to be perfect for the job."

"What makes you think he's involved with the cactus thefts?" Fenton asked.

Grish seemed annoyed as he said, "Time, partly. The thefts started just a few days after Kidwell was hired. And don't forget he has the background and skills to be able to dig up large plants without hurting them. Also, he discovered most of the vandalized sites, including the one we saw today, even when he had a work assignment in a different section of the park."

13

"Why would that make him a suspect?" Frank asked. "If he was involved in the crimes, wouldn't he want someone else to discover them?"

"He's trying to look innocent," Grish said. "But I'm not buying it. I'm hoping to catch him and his accomplices in the act, but I haven't been able to figure out whom he's working with yet."

"What makes you think he has accomplices?" Joe asked.

"Because the specimens he's taken are large," Grish answered. "Removing them requires heavy equipment, and I doubt that one person could do it alone."

"Who's handling the investigation?" Fenton asked.

"I'm supposed to be working in conjunction with the state investigators in Phoenix," Grish said. "But so far they've been swamped with other cases and haven't been able to make a trip out here."

"So who is helping you?" Joe asked.

"I've been pretty much on my own," Grish said, braking to avoid hitting a jackrabbit. "I check the sites myself as soon as we find them. I take photographs, make measurements, keep records, that sort of thing. Gather evidence."

"Have you checked on Kidwell's background to see if he has a record?" Frank asked.

"I didn't think of that," Grish said.

"I'm sure all this interferes with your other duties," Fenton said.

"Yes, it does," Grish said with a nod. "But it's part of my job."

"What about the tourists?" Frank asked. "Don't people notice the holes in the ground and the damage from the trucks running over the plants?"

"Sometimes," Grish said. "If they report anything, we tell them that, yes, there has been some damage and we are investigating. That's all they need to hear."

"Well, it sounds to me as if you could use a little help," Joe said. "We—"

"I appreciate the offer," Grish said, glancing at Joe in the rearview mirror. "But why don't you relax, enjoy yourselves, and take in the sights?"

As he turned the car into the campground, Grish became quiet. They drove between rows of large motor homes, each parked at a designated campsite with a picnic table beside it. Couples and families sat around the table at most of the sites.

"Some of these campers look as if they've been here for a while," Fenton said.

"Some of them stay for weeks," Grish said. "Most move on after a day or two, though."

"Have any of them been here for longer than a few weeks?" Joe asked.

Grish nodded as he pulled up behind the Hardys' motor home. "As a matter of fact, this guy right next to you has been here quite a while. His name is Townsend. He's a university professor. He and his daughter are doing biological research of some

15

kind—she's his assistant. She's nice enough, but he's a little hard to talk to. They aren't here all the time, though. They leave for a couple of days every week or two."

"Is there anybody besides Kidwell who might be involved in the cactus thefts?" Joe asked. "Any of the tourists?"

"No," Grish said. "But listen. I know you're dying to get involved. I'm sure you are all very good detectives, but I don't want word of my suspicions to get out. There are just too many big ears around."

"Grish, we are experienced investigators," Frank said, "and we know how to keep our mouths shut. We could be a lot of help to you."

Fenton joined in and said, "That's true. It's your business, if you don't want our help. But you know as well as we do that we can keep things confidential."

Grish turned around in his seat and said, "I appreciate the offer, but let me handle it. If I need help, you'll be the first to know. Now, if you'll excuse me, I have work to do at the office."

Putting the car into gear, Grish paused. "This job used to be fun," he said. "Now we're looking at budget cuts, downsizing, people losing their jobs, and now all this thievery. I'm getting tired. Is that dinner invitation still open?"

"We'll be waiting for you," Fenton said.

As the Hardys got out of the car, Grish said, "Great. And if you come by the office in the

16

morning, I'll show you a map of the very best places to see in the park."

He drove away. Frank and Joe watched him go, then looked at each other.

"Now, guys," Fenton said with amusement, "I know that look in your eyes. But you've got to remember, this is Grish's concern. Let's do as he asks and stay out of it. If he wants help, he'll ask."

"Right, Dad," Joe said, with a wink at Frank. "It sounds interesting, though. Cactus rustlers?"

"It does," Fenton said as he took a seat at the picnic table. "In the meantime, who's cooking? I'm starved."

"It's Joe's turn to cook," Frank said, taking a seat beside him.

"That's right," Joe said. "Tonight we'll be having Joe Hardy's Gourmet Beans and Wienies."

"The last time we had Joe Hardy's Beans and Wienies," Frank said with a laugh, "they were burned to a crisp."

"That," Joe said, opening the door of the motor home, "is because you weren't paying attention when I stepped out and asked you to watch them." He disappeared inside to get the food and drinks, then poked his head out for a moment.

"I love this motor home," he said. "I still can't get over it. It's got a bathroom, beds, a dining room, and a living room with a TV. It even has a complete kitchen. It's just like a house on wheels. Hey, we could go into business selling wienies and live out here like real cowboys. Wouldn't that be great?"

17

"Yeah, right, dude," Frank said, rolling his eyes. "We're your first customers, and we're not terribly impressed with the service."

"Hey, you just gave me an idea, Frank," Joe said. "We could call our company Food for Dudes! What do you think?"

Fenton laughed. Frank shook his head and said, "Dream on, bro."

Fenton had rented the motor home in Phoenix on their way to Organ Pipe, and at first the feeling of driving a house down the road was strange. But they'd adjusted quickly, enjoying the idea that whoever was not driving could walk to the refrigerator anytime to get a cold drink or even work out with the weights they'd brought along.

At the dealer's suggestion, they had also rented a small car to tow. That way, once they got to Organ Pipe, they could leave the motor home parked at the campground and drive around in the car. And since the motor home came equipped with a two-way CB radio, Fenton had also rented a CB walkie-talkie to keep in the car.

Frank opened an outside cabinet door on the side of the motor home and pulled out a bag of charcoal. As he sprinkled the chunks in the raised brick barbecue, he said, "You know, Dad, I was thinking. Joe and I could work on this case while we're here, and Grish wouldn't even have to know about it."

"Oh?" Fenton said, popping open a can of soda.

"If we could figure out where the other theft sites have been," Frank continued, "we could do

18

our own investigating. This park covers thousands of square miles, so Grish wouldn't even see us. We could get tire measurements, check out the damage, look for footprints, whatever. Plus, we could get to know some of the people here at the campground and get a feeling for whether any of them are involved. I'll bet there are clues Grish has missed."

"That's right," Joe said. He had come back out and was trying to light the charcoal. "I don't think he has any training in detective work."

"And he wouldn't have to know we were involved until after we've solved the case," Frank said. "Dad, you could visit with him and keep him busy while we check things out. Meanwhile, we can trail Kidwell to figure out what he's up to, and we can call to find out if he has a criminal record. And while you're hanging out with Grish, he might even accidentally give you some information we could use for solving the case."

"Grish has asked us to stay out of this affair," Fenton reminded Frank. "We don't want to cause any trouble for him. Personally, I think he can probably solve this case on his own, given enough time."

Joe was admiring the flames curling around the charcoal when he noticed that a young man had squatted down behind the Hardys' motor home, almost out of view. He was pointing a camera at a small cactus near the right rear tire, but his eyes were on the Hardys. As soon as Joe spotted him, he straightened up and started fiddling with his camera. He looked about eighteen or nineteen, tall and thin, with a long blond ponytail. Joe had a strong hunch he'd been eavesdropping.

"Excuse me," Joe called loudly. "What are you doing? Do you need something?" Joe walked around the corner of the motor home, a frown on his face.

The man turned and walked off, as if Joe hadn't even spoken.

"Hey!" Joe shouted. "I asked you what you were doing."

At that, the man took off, running fast in the other direction. And just as fast, Joe was after him.

3 A Suspect Arrives

Sprinting after the intruder, Joe caught up with him two campsites away. He grabbed his arm and pulled him to a stop, whirling the guy around to face him.

"Take your hands off me!" the man exclaimed, struggling against Joe's firm grip. "You've got no—"

"What's the deal?" Joe said. "Why were you spying on us like that?"

"I wasn't spying," the man said. "I was taking some shots of that cactus by your motor home. Let go of my arm!"

Realizing that other campers were watching curiously, Joe released the man but stayed poised for another sprint. Just then Frank caught up to them.

"Who are you?" he demanded. "Why were you spying on us?"

"I just told this other guy, I wasn't spying," the man insisted again. "My name is Raymond Perez. I'm a landscape painter. Perhaps you've heard of me?"

"No," Frank said. "We haven't."

Perez looked a bit wounded at that. "Well," he went on, "I take pictures of objects and scenes I want to use as subjects for paintings. I was shooting that cactus when you startled me."

"Why did you run?" Joe asked.

"Because of the tone in your voice when you shouted," Perez said. "Wouldn't you run, if someone yelled at you that way?"

Joe smiled confidently and said, "I don't think so."

"You still haven't said why you were listening to our conversation," Frank said.

"I told you, I was not listening," Perez said, his voice rising angrily. "I was trying to take a picture. I'm shooting that plant at different times of the day, because the light changes and it looks slightly different each time. But now," he added, waving his hand, "you've spoiled it. The light is different and I've lost my chance."

Joe glanced around at the sky. "I guess the color of the light is your business," he said, "but next time, announce yourself."

Perez smiled and said, "You mean so you can stop talking about whatever's such a secret?"

"I thought you said you weren't eavesdropping," Joe said.

"I wasn't," Perez replied, "but I did catch a few words. What was that you were saying about a case you want to solve? Are you guys detectives or something?"

Grish was right about the tourists having big ears, Frank realized. "You must have heard us wrong," he said, then tried to change the subject. "So, are you an expert on desert plants? Or do you just take pictures of them when the light is pink?"

Perez grinned. "I get it," he said. "You're cleverly changing the subject so you don't have to answer my question. That tells me you probably *are* detectives, in which case you must be working under cover and don't want me to blow your cover."

A glance at his brother's face told Frank that Joe didn't know what to make of Perez either.

"Who are you, anyway, since you don't want to tell me whether you are detectives?" Perez inquired.

"I'm Frank Hardy and this is my brother, Joe," Frank said.

"Nice to meet you," Perez said, shaking hands. "And to answer your earlier question, no, I'm not an expert on cactus or anything. I'm just an artist, lost in the desert. I want to do a painting of that cactus at your campsite and call it *Nature Hangs In There*. That plant has put up with so much, and it's still hanging in there. You'd think by now somebody would have run it over or kicked it accidentally or something."

Joe laughed and said, "I hope your paintings are better than your titles. How long have you been staying here?"

"A couple of months, off and on," Perez said. "The place gets a little dull, if you know what I mean. I head back to California every couple of weeks for a few days. But overall, I've been here longer than just about anybody. Even longer than that old professor in the campsite next to yours."

"You mean Professor Townsend?" Joe asked.

"Yeah, him," Perez replied. "He's a crab, but his daughter is nice. Her name is Diane."

"What does the professor do here?" Joe asked.

"I don't know," Perez said. "He— Hey, why are we standing out here in the middle of the road? You guys want to come over to my place and have a soda? It's right over there."

The three walked over to Perez's campsite as he continued to talk about Professor Townsend. "I'm not sure what he does around here," Perez said. "He and Diane go off almost every day. I see them here and there in the park. Or rather I see their truck pulled over on the side of the road. I guess they're out in the desert someplace, doing research or something. I tried to talk to him one day about what he does, but he almost snapped my head off."

"What about Diane?" Frank asked. "Is she easier to talk to?"

Perez shrugged. "I guess," he said. "But she seems a little afraid of him."

"What do you mean?" Frank asked.

"I mean she clams up when he's around," Perez said.

When they reached Perez's campsite, Joe saw litter under the picnic table—a banana peel and some used paper plates. Maybe he's a famous artist, Joe thought wryly, but he needs to learn some housekeeping skills. And he doesn't seem to have much respect for the great outdoors.

"Does Diane talk much when her dad isn't around?" Frank asked.

"Yeah, I guess," Perez said, opening an ice chest. "You guys want a cola? That's all I've got."

"No, thanks," Joe said.

"A cola would be fine," Frank said. "So, what does Diane have to say when her dad isn't around?"

Perez handed a cold, wet can to Frank and said, "Well, she told me he's doing some kind of medical research. Something to do with using cacti and other desert plants as sources for medicine. I couldn't get her to be more specific than that. I do know they leave every few days, always at night."

"At night?" Frank asked.

"Yeah," Perez said. "They take off about sunset in their pickup, and they leave the camp trailer behind. They come back a day or two later."

"When was the last time they left?" Joe asked.

Perez looked thoughtful for a moment. "Three days ago," he said. "They came back about noon today, just before you arrived."

"Man," Joe said, "you notice everything, don't you?"

Perez brightened. "Arists are observant. I keep my eyes and ears open. That way I don't miss any of the action."

"Who else besides you and Professor Townsend has been here for a long time?" Frank asked.

Perez thought for a moment. "Nobody, really," he said. "There's a couple down on the end who were here for a week and then gone for maybe a month. I think they were in Mexico. They've been back about a week now. But that's about it. Everybody else is just passing through, more or less."

Frank looked carefully at Perez, trying to guess what he was thinking. Frank wondered if he was just a busybody or if his nosiness had some other purpose. "Well," Frank said, "we'd better get back. Joe, I think you've got some hot dogs to put on the grill. That charcoal should be the right temperature by now." He shook hands with Perez. "Thanks for the soda."

On the way back to their campsite, Frank said, "That guy could be a good source of information if we need it."

Joe nodded. "But I'm not sure I trust him," he

said. "For somebody who is trying to focus on his art, he seems to know an awful lot about other people's business."

"True," Frank said. "We'll have to keep a close watch on him. I think there is more to Raymond Perez than meets the eye."

Fenton was inside the motor home when they arrived, washing his hands at the sink.

When Joe and Frank stepped inside the door, Fenton said, "Well, I'm glad you boys got back in one piece. What happened with our eavesdropper?"

Frank and Joe told Fenton about their conversation with Perez, and Fenton agreed that Perez needed watching. "But in the meantime," he said, "somebody better get out there and do some cooking or I'm going to starve to death."

"Right, Dad," Joe said, heading for the door. "Time for some dude food."

After Joe set the hot dogs and the pot of beans on the grill, he dusted off the table. Just as Frank emerged from the motor home with plates and silverware, Kidwell drove by in his blue pickup.

"Hmm," Frank said. He set out the silverware and plates on the table. "I wonder what he's up to."

"I don't know," Joe said, "but I have a feeling it's something."

"Are you thinking what I'm thinking?" Frank asked.

"Follow him?" Joe asked.

"Yup," Frank said. "Let's go."

"Hey, Dad," Joe called through the door of the motor home. "Watch the hot dogs. We'll be back in a minute."

Frank started the car and sped up until he came within sight of the blue pickup.

"Hang back," Joe said. "We don't want him to spot us."

"Right," Frank said, slowing to keep some distance from the truck. "He seems to be headed to the office."

"That's what I would guess," Joe said.

They followed as the pickup led them another half mile down the curving road to Grish's office. Kidwell pulled up beside the office and got out. Frank stopped the car far enough back so that Kidwell didn't seem to notice them as he walked into the office. Then Frank drove on and parked the car on the other side of the building.

"Now what?" Joe asked.

"I'm not sure," Frank said. "I guess we wait to see what happens. It's getting dark, so we can follow him when he leaves."

"Yeah," Joe said. "If he's the cactus thief, he might just head to some other part of the park to steal another one."

"He won't be loading a giant cactus into that little pickup," Frank said.

"No," Joe said. "But maybe he'll have a rendezvous with his accomplices. You know, I was thinking—"

At that moment they heard someone yell angrily from inside the office. A second man shouted, and Frank and Joe exchanged a glance, recognizing the voice as Grisham's.

Then they heard glass shattering.

4 A Midnight Adventure

"Let's go!" Joe said, throwing open his door. Together he and Frank raced for the office. Joe reached the door first and opened it.

Kidwell had Grish backed up against the wall, with a grip on the ranger's shirt. The younger man's fist was raised, ready to slug Grish. Kidwell looked around as the Hardys entered. His grip on the ranger slowly relaxed as he realized what he was doing, and after a few tense seconds he released Grish.

"What's going on?" Joe asked.

The men looked away from each other, straightening their clothing. "It's over," Grish said. "Everybody's okay. Mr. Kidwell and I just had a little disagreement. Right, David?" Grish let out his breath slowly and said, "Frank and Joe, why don't you two wait outside for a moment?" He waved toward the door.

Frank exchanged glances with Joe, then followed him outside, shutting the door behind them.

"What do you suppose that was all about?" Joe asked.

"Who knows?" Frank said. "It probably had to do with what happened this afternoon on the road."

Another shout came from inside, but before the Hardys could decide whether to interfere, the door flew open and Kidwell stomped out. He turned and shouted, "And you know what I'm talking about!" Then he marched straight to his pickup, got in, started the engine, and drove away, spinning his tires as he went.

Inside the office, Grish was sitting at his desk. He looked up as Frank and Joe entered. "I'm not sure what made you boys show up when you did," he said, "but I guess it was a good thing. Kidwell and I were about to go at it." Grish smoothed back his sandy hair and wiped his brow.

"What happened?" Frank asked.

Grish explained that when he'd said something to Kidwell about his irresponsible driving, Kidwell had come after him.

Joe asked whether Grish had mentioned the shovel.

"I did bring up the shovel," Grish said, nodding. "But as soon as I mentioned it, he blew up. And then, after you left the office, I tried again to talk to

31

him. When I mentioned the shovel, he up and quit his job. Just like that."

"What did he mean when he said you knew what he was talking about?" Frank asked.

Grish spread his hands. "I wish I knew," he said. "That's the puzzle. I mentioned his driving and then the shovel. And I just barely touched on that."

"That doesn't make any sense," Joe said.

"You're right," Grish said. "Anyway, after all of this, I'm not feeling very sociable. I'd like a rain check on dinner, if you don't mind."

"Sure thing," Frank said. "We totally understand. Besides, the hot dogs Joe was fixing are either burned to a crisp, if Dad forgot to watch them, or else they're ice cold."

"Good thing the motor home has a microwave," Joe said. "If the wieners are cold, we can reheat 'em in the nuke box."

Grish smiled wryly. "Sounds delicious," he said, "but I'll pass." He reminded them to come by with Fenton in the morning. "I'll give you guys a map and instructions for finding the best hiking and climbing spots in the park," he said.

"I think Grish needs our help more than we thought," Joe said as Frank drove them back to the campground. "But what are we going to do about Kidwell? It'll be kind of tough to keep an eye on him now that he's quit."

"Tough, if not impossible," Frank said.

As Frank pulled the car into the campsite, Joe

suddenly said, "Whoa, Frank. Back up and shine the headlights over that way." He pointed toward Professor Townsend's truck, which was parked at the next campsite. Frank backed the car around and shone the beams toward the truck.

"Hold it right there," Joe said. Something shaped like a log, about two feet long and four inches thick, was lying under the truck. Joe got out and looked more closely. In the glare of the headlights, he could see that the object was actually the broken-off limb of an organ pipe. He reached under the truck and tried to grasp the limb without getting thorns in his fingers.

"Hey! What are you doing?" A man's voice came from the trailer parked beside the truck.

Must be Professor Townsend, Joe thought, straightening up. "Sorry," he said. "I didn't mean to bother you, but there seems to be a big piece of cactus under your truck. I was just trying to pull it out."

"What do you mean, a piece of cactus?" Townsend asked. He stepped out of the trailer and closed the door behind him. He was a tall, gray-haired man with stooped shoulders, and he squinted in the glare from the headlights. "Why are you interested in a piece of cactus under my truck?" He walked around to look. As soon as he realized what Joe was pointing at, he stiffened. "Young man," he said, "I think you should mind your own business."

"But don't you—"

"I've made myself clear," the professor said. "But let me repeat my advice: mind your own business."

The door to Townsend's trailer opened, and a young woman peeked out. She looked about eighteen, and had long, dark hair. "Dad," she said, "is something wrong?"

"Everything is fine, Diane," Townsend said. "I'll take care of it. You stay inside." Turning to Joe, he said, "I think you should go back to wherever you belong."

"I belong right next door," Joe said. "My name is Joe Hardy, and I guess we—my dad and my brother and I—are your neighbors. Are you Professor Townsend?"

Joe extended his hand, but Townsend did not take it. "How did you know my name?" he asked.

"We asked someone," Joe said, and with his brightest smile added, "We like to get to know our neighbors."

Frank got out of the car and strode over, leaving the engine running and the headlights on. "This is my brother, Frank," Joe said.

Frank extended his hand, but Townsend again ignored the gesture. "Professor, isn't that a piece of organ pipe cactus under your truck?" Frank asked.

"I'm not sure," Townsend said. "As I said, I'll take care of it, and you two can go home."

"How did—" Frank said, but Townsend cut him off.

"I said go home!" Townsend exclaimed. "This is my campsite, and I'll take care of whatever happens in it."

Fenton came around the corner of the Hardys' motor home. "What's going on here?" he asked. "What's all the yelling about?"

"Is this a party?" Townsend asked, his voice rising. "Who invited all you people?" To Fenton he said, "Are you with these boys?"

"I'm their father, Fenton Hardy. What's going on?"

"What's going on?" Townsend asked in a loud voice. "I have asked these young men to leave, and I would appreciate your assistance in the matter. And please turn off the lights on your vehicle. They are quite irritating."

Frank went to the car and shut off the lights. "No problem," he said. "Joe, Dad, I think we should let the professor take care of the cactus."

Joe recognized a certain tone in Frank's voice, and said, "Okay. Sure. Sorry to bother you, Professor." He and Fenton walked back to their motor home while Frank pulled the car into the parking space. Then the three of them went into the motor home and shut the door behind them.

"Quick," Frank said, "turn off all the lights except at the back end." Joe did as Frank asked. Once the lights were out, Frank peeked through a window at the front of the motor home to see what Professor Townsend would do.

"He's wrapping the cactus limb in a blanket," Frank said. "Now he's putting it in his pickup." Frank watched as Townsend started up his truck and drove off into the night.

"The professor was in a real hurry," Frank said. "He wrapped up that cactus as if he'd done it a hundred times before. Then he got it out of here quick."

"He seems to be concealing something," Fenton said.

"Yes, but what?" Frank asked. "He's supposedly an expert on the desert, and he's got to know that it's against the law to disturb the cacti out here. That could be why he was so upset that we spotted the limb under his pickup."

"It might have gotten caught under his truck somehow while he was driving around," Joe said. "But why would somebody like him be off-roading in the desert?"

"Maybe for his research," Frank said. "Or maybe he's involved with the cactus thieves. Somehow he doesn't seem like the type to get his hands dirty transplanting big plants."

"No," Joe said, "but he could be the mastermind behind the rustling. He sure did act upset when we saw that thing under his truck."

"Hey, we're pretty good, aren't we?" Frank said. "So far we've turned up three suspects—Kidwell, Perez, and the prof—and we haven't even been here twelve hours."

"And in those twelve hours, I haven't eaten a

36

bite," Fenton said. "Are you interested in salvaging those gourmet hot dogs you left on the grill, Joe?"

"Oh, my gosh!" Joe said, jumping for the door. "I forgot the dude dogs!"

"Hold it!" Fenton called. "They're in the fridge. I brought them in when they were done and you still weren't back. I rescued the beans, too."

After wolfing down a late dinner, Joe began to feel drowsy. The fresh desert air was making him pleasantly tired, and he climbed gratefully into his sleeping bag on his bunk. Drifting off, he could hear the sounds that Grish had promised—the high-pitched songs of the coyotes, calling from one direction and being answered from another, under the stars in the chilly night air. He smiled and fell asleep.

He was awakened about one o'clock by a distant sound he couldn't identify at first. Listening for a few more moments, he realized he was hearing the revving of a big engine, like that of a slow-moving truck. The sound was coming from the west, though, not from the direction of the highway.

He got up and tapped Frank's shoulder. "Listen," he whispered. "What does that sound like to you?"

Frank rubbed his eyes and listened. "Engines," he whispered back. "Only"—he sat up—"from the wrong direction."

"Exactly," Joe whispered. "The highway through the park is to the east of us. A vehicle on that highway would be moving fast, and the sound would fade away. What we're hearing is steady, like a vehicle sitting in one place with the engine running."

"Like a truck running a winch," Frank whispered.

"Maybe," Joe whispered, glancing over to see if their father was stirring. "It could be the cactus thieves."

"Let's check it out," Frank whispered.

They pulled on their jeans, sweatshirts, and hiking boots, and tiptoed out the door. But as they started across the campground, Frank had an afterthought. "Let's wake up Dad to tell him where we're going," he said. "We can turn on the CB radio and take the walkie-talkie from the car. Then if we get out there and actually catch the thieves in the act, we can radio back to Dad, and he can get hold of Grish."

"Good idea," Joe said. They woke Fenton, explained what they were up to, and turned on the radio in the motor home. Grabbing the CB walkie-talkie from the car, they started hiking across the desert in the direction of the vehicle sounds.

The terrain was uneven and the footing a little tricky, even in the bright moonlight. Other than the engine noise the night was quiet, so they were able to head straight for the sounds. But after a while it seemed as if they weren't getting any closer.

Frank stopped. "You know what?" he said. "I can't hear the engines anymore."

Joe stopped to listen. "Me neither," he said.

"Maybe they shut down for a few minutes. Think we should keep going?"

"I don't know," Frank said. He looked around at the moonlit desert landscape. With no city lights in the background, the stars were brilliant against the black sky. The nocturnal animals must have been scared off by the noise, Frank thought, because I don't see or hear another living creature out here. "Maybe we should check in with Dad," he whispered to his brother.

"Good idea," Joe said, "assuming he hasn't fallen back to sleep." Joe switched on the CB, adjusting the gain to cut down the hiss. As he was about to transmit, a man's voice cut in on the channel.

"You headin' out?" the voice said.

After a pause, a second voice said, "Roger that. The job's done, and we got a good one. Think I'll take the rest of the night off."

"Okay," the first voice said. "Catch you at the place."

"Roger that," the second voice said. "Out."

Joe waited a few seconds to see if there would be any more talk, then turned the radio off. "Are you thinking what I'm thinking?" he asked his brother.

"You mean, maybe those were the voices of the cactus thieves?" Frank said.

"That's exactly what I was thinking."

"What channel was that?" Frank asked.

"Channel ten," Joe said. "Let's remember it."

When they returned to the motor home a few minutes later, they filled Fenton in on their late-night hike and told him what they'd heard over the CB.

He suggested they not jump to conclusions about whether the voices had come from the cactus thieves. "I'm sure lots of truckers go up and down the highway through the park," he said, "or it could have been local workers heading home from their jobs. We'll tell Grish about it tomorrow."

After breakfast the next morning they drove to the head ranger's office and let themselves in. Grish was talking to a man who looked like a real live cowboy. He was tall and wiry, and wore a broad-brimmed ten-gallon hat. Joe noticed that his face was deeply lined from years in the sun.

Grish waved to them as he finished his conversation with the cowboy. "I'm usually here in the office until six or seven," he said to the man, "although the sign says we close at five. We need to work together to keep those cattle of yours out of the park."

"You're right," the man said. "We'll have to see what we can do." He nodded to the Hardys as he walked out.

After the man was gone, Grish said, "Good morning. I trust you all slept well?"

"It was okay," Fenton said. "A lot of coyote howling, just as you said."

"Didn't I tell you?" Grish said. "For me it's like a lullaby. I drop off to sleep almost as soon as I hear

40

it. So are you ready to check out some of our scenic wonders?"

"Not yet," Frank said. "We need to tell you that our next-door neighbor, Professor Townsend, may have something to hide."

Grish grew serious. "What do you mean?"

Frank told him about their encounter with Townsend and how the professor had gotten rid of the cactus limb.

Grish nodded. "Hmm," he said. "I guess I need to have a talk with him."

"He's at his campsite now," Joe said, "but I think he and his daughter are getting ready to go somewhere. They were putting some things in their truck when we left."

Grish stood up. "I'd better move on this, then," he said. "I'll have to meet with you later."

"No problem," Joe said, thinking he'd tell the ranger about the previous night's activities when he next saw him. He and Frank and Fenton got into the car and went back to the campground. They were waiting at the picnic table when Grish arrived. Professor Townsend, with Diane seated beside him, was backing the truck out of the parking space.

Grish jumped out of his truck and held up a hand for Townsend to stop. Townsend rolled down his window. "What can I do for you?" he asked.

"I have a report that a contraband desert plant was found under your truck last night," Grish said. "What can you tell me about it?"

Townsend fired an angry look at Frank and Joe. "I knew it!" he shouted. "Didn't I tell you, Diane? They're a pair of liars! And I'm going to make sure they regret it." Townsend threw his truck into gear and sped away, showering Grish with gravel and dust.

Grish turned his face away from the truck to avoid getting flying gravel in his eyes. The pickup disappeared from view, leaving dust in its wake. "Now, there," he said, "is an attitude problem."

5 On the Trail

"Man, oh, man," Joe said, looking at the cloud of dust that was all that was left of Townsend's fleeing truck. "That guy sure is acting awfully guilty."

"He must have something to hide," Frank added.

Fenton nodded. "Why would he be so testy about that cactus?" he said. "Today he was even worse than he was last night."

"Don't mind him," Grish said. "He's under a lot of pressure. The university is threatening to cut off his research funding if he doesn't come up with something soon. His daughter told me he's spent years on this project. And if the university cuts off his funding, he'll be out of a job."

"So he's feeling a lot of pressure about money," Frank stated. "Do you suppose he could be working with Kidwell? Have you ever seen them together?"

43

Grish shook his head. "I haven't seen them consorting, but that doesn't mean anything. This is a big park, and by now they both know their way around it. There are a thousand places they could get together without being seen."

"And then there's Raymond Perez," Joe said.

"Perez?" Grish asked. "The artist?"

"He knows about the thefts, and we caught him eavesdropping near our campsite," Frank explained.

"And then there are those desert creatures that only come out at night," Joe said, "to talk on their CBs."

"What's this about CBs?" Grish said, his eyebrows going up.

Frank and Joe told him about the hike they'd taken in the middle of the night and about hearing an engine and something like sentry instructions on the CB.

"I know Perez," Grish said. "He's been staying here for a while. He's always into something, like a little kid." He pursed his lips thoughtfully for a moment. "But CBs? These guys must be more sophisticated than I thought," he said. "If they're using radios, it will be even harder to catch them in the act."

"You'll need some good solid detective work," Joe said.

Grish looked at him keenly and then smiled. "I know you'd like to work on the case, Joe," he said, "and now I'm thinking, with this new information about the CB radio, maybe that wouldn't be such a bad idea. You two could be my eyes and ears. You've already turned up, what, two more suspects in your first day? That's pretty quick work. If I let you get involved, though, you have to make me a promise."

"What's that?" Joe said.

"That you'll keep me informed of everything you discover. That way I'll feel that I'm still in charge and following the rules. Is it a deal?"

"Deal," Joe said.

"It's a deal," Frank said. "You're the boss."

Grish turned to Fenton. "How about you, old buddy?" he asked.

"You've got my word," Fenton said. "But this trip is a vacation for me, and I plan on relaxing. Frank and Joe can do all the legwork, and I'll supervise."

"No, *I'll* supervise," Grish said with a laugh. "You can visit with me."

"Now, that's an offer I have to accept," Fenton said. "So, why don't we head over to your office? You can give us a map of the park and show us where the thefts have taken place."

"And we can talk about Kidwell," Frank said, "and the other suspects."

Frank and Joe drove the car to the office, with Fenton and Grish following in Grish's truck. When they arrived, Kidwell's blue pickup was parked outside the office, and Kidwell was sitting on the steps, waiting.

"There's our man," Frank said to Joe. "He must be here to try to get his job back."

Grish and Fenton pulled up next to Kidwell's truck. The ranger got out and said, "Morning, David. What's up?"

Kidwell stood up and looked from the Hardys to Grish. "I think we need to talk," he said.

"I think so, too," Grish said. "Would you mind waiting out here for a few minutes?" he said to the Hardys. They nodded. "Thanks," said Grish, and he and Kidwell went into the office and closed the door. Frank and Joe stood beside the steps, and Fenton leaned on Grish's truck.

Joe said, "Do you think Grish will give him his job back, after Kidwell attacked him like that?"

"I'm not sure I would," Fenton said. "But maybe Grish knows something we don't know. Maybe Kidwell is under some kind of personal pressure."

"Or maybe Grish wants to have Kidwell around so we can keep an eye on him," Frank said.

Joe stepped up onto the porch and strolled past the window. Inside, Grish was sitting at his desk, with Kidwell standing on the other side. Kidwell was talking earnestly about something while Grish listened, his hands folded.

"It looks like they're really talking," Joe said. "I think Grish is going to give him another chance."

"Good," Frank said. "That means we can keep an eye on him."

"You know, I was thinking about that," Fenton

said. "If the cactus thieves work mainly at night to avoid being seen, then Kidwell and his accomplices probably won't do anything incriminating in the daylight."

"He might scout around during the day for specimens to steal," Frank said.

"Yes, he might," Fenton said. "In which case you guys might want to tail him. On the other hand, it might be more worthwhile to spend some time thoroughly checking out the other theft sites."

"Maybe Grish will have them laid out on a map," Joe said.

The office door opened, and Kidwell walked out. Without looking at the Hardys, he strode straight to his truck, got in, and drove away.

When the Hardys went inside, Grish said, "Well, I decided to let him stay on. He apologized for blowing up yesterday and said he really needed the job. Since he put it that way, I said yes. I was also thinking that he'll be easier to track if he's still working here."

"That's what we were thinking, too," Frank said. "Do you know where he's headed? Joe and I can catch up with him and keep an eye on what he does."

"I'll show you on the map," Grish said.

"And while you're at it," Joe said, "why don't you give us an idea of where the thefts have occurred, so we can look at those sites?"

"As a matter of fact," Grish said, "I told David to

47

clean up one of the vandalized areas this morning. We've been trying to repair them as quickly as we can."

He reached into a drawer and pulled out a map of Organ Pipe Cactus National Monument. Unfolding it on his desk, he said, "This is a topographic map. As you probably know, all these squiggly lines show how steep the terrain is, so you can tell where the mountains are, the flattest places, and so forth."

"We've worked with topo maps before," Joe said. "These long heavy lines circling through the park must be the roads. There's only one for the whole western part of the park."

"Show us where the cactus thefts have occurred," Frank said.

Grish paused, then got up and went to another map on the wall. "I'll mark the sites with red dots. Let's see. There have been eighteen different sites. Most have been in the northwest quadrant of the park, where there's less traffic."

Frank peered over Grish's shoulder and asked, "Where's the one we saw yesterday? Wasn't it in this area?" He pointed to a section of the park on the east side.

"I think it was about here," Grish said, tapping the map. "Near the Diablo Mountains. I guess I'll mark that, too." He marked another dot on the map. "That makes nineteen."

"Where's Kidwell working this morning?" Joe asked.

Grish pointed to a red dot in the northwest quadrant. "Here."

Joe marked the same spot on his map with a pen, then asked, "And he's headed up that way now?"

"He's supposed to be," Grish said, returning to his desk. "Now, remember," he said. "You guys are to keep me posted on what happens. I'll include it all in my reports."

"No problem," Joe said.

Frank, looking at the map in front of Joe, said, "I've been trying to figure out where those sounds we heard last night could have been coming from. It had to be somewhere out here, in the western part of the park."

"We'll head past there on our way to check on Kidwell," Joe said. "We can keep our eyes open for tracks leading off the road."

"Good idea," Fenton said. "You guys be careful. Understand?"

"Sure, Dad," Joe said. "Ready to hit the trail, Frank?" As Joe reached for the door, Raymond Perez walked in with a big smile on his face.

"Say, guys," he said. "What's up?"

"Oh, not much," Joe said. He looked meaningfully at Frank and nodded toward the door, in a gesture that said, Let's get out of here.

Perez's smile broadened. "Well, guess what?" he said.

"What?" Joe said, his eyes still on Frank.

"You'll never guess," Perez said.

Joe sighed impatiently. Frank finished folding the map and started for the door.

Behind Perez's back, Joe waved goodbye to his father and Grish and started to sneak out the door. He froze at Perez's next words.

"I just found the spot where someone stole a cactus last night," Perez said.

6 Getting Too Close

"What?" Joe yelled. Grish stood up.

Perez laughed and repeated himself. "I said I just found the spot where a cactus was stolen last night."

"Who told you about people stealing cacti?" Grish said, his face stern.

"I figured something was going on," Perez said. "I've seen a couple of strange things, places torn up around the park. I reported that one place a couple of weeks ago. Remember, Grish? You said you already knew about it? Then I overheard these two guys talking last night"—Perez pointed to Frank and Joe—"and I figured there must be a major investigation happening."

So much for working under cover, Joe thought with frustration as Perez continued.

"And then I was channel-surfing in the middle of the night on my CB scanner," Perez said. "I picked up a transmission about getting a cactus framed up and loaded. I figured it must have been the bad guys in action. I didn't have any way to get a fix on their location, but I could hear some engine sounds off to the northwest. I know this park like the back of my hand, so this morning I drove out to where I figured the sounds were coming from. Sure enough, I found a big hole." Perez grinned.

Grish looked exasperated. "Listen, Perez, this is part of an ongoing investigation. Things are kind of delicate right now because . . . well, for various reasons. I'd appreciate it if you'd mind your own business."

Ignoring Grish and looking from Frank to Joe, Perez said, "So you guys really are detectives."

"Did you hear me, Perez?" Grish said. "I said butt out."

"Okay," Perez said, looking disappointed and angry. "I can see when I'm not wanted." He started out the door, stopping when Frank put a hand on his arm.

"Before you go," Frank said, "tell us where the spot is."

"Aha!" Perez exclaimed, his face lighting up again. "Do I get to play spy, too?"

"Just tell us where the place is," Frank said as patiently as he could.

"Are you going to let me in on the fun," Perez asked, "or do I take my ball and go home?"

"We can probably find that spot ourselves," Joe said with a shrug, "just as you did, Perez. Let's get out of here, Frank."

"But we could save time," Frank said, "if Perez showed us what he found. He could be a big help."

"A big help?" Grish repeated. "What about the confidentiality of this case? If Perez knows, who's next?"

"Hang on," Frank said. "Perez has already figured out about the cactus thefts, right? And he's kept his mouth shut so far. Right, Perez?"

Perez's eyes were alight with excitement. "Absolutely," he insisted. "Hey," he said to Grish, "all I want to do is help. To do my duty as an American citizen to protect federal land and innocent cacti everywhere."

Frank could feel himself starting to like Perez. He was clever, and Frank realized it might be fun to have him on their team. But Grish wanted to maintain complete control of the investigation, and he clearly didn't want Perez involved.

"Grish," Frank said, "I don't think you have anything to worry about. Joe and I will keep an eye on Perez. Think of it this way: at least we'll know where he is most of the time, so he can't get into trouble."

Grish shook his head. "Whatever," he said finally. "I give up. This is turning into a circus anyway. Just remember that I need to keep track of everything in my reports. The guys from the state are going to be here pretty soon, and I have to have everything down in writing. Understood?"

"It's a deal," Frank said. "Let's get on the trail." He held the door open as Joe and Perez walked out, then waved to his father and left.

The three of them piled into the car, with Joe driving and Perez in the backseat.

"Okay, Perez," Frank said. "Which way?"

Perez directed them to an area about four miles northwest of the campground. "It's right up here," he said after a few minutes. "On the left."

Joe slowed until he came to some tire tracks leading away from the road. He pulled over and shut off the engine. "Would you look at that?" he said. "They really trashed this place, didn't they?"

"You aren't kidding," Frank said. Large, dual-tire tracks led off from the shoulder of the road, marked by squashed bushes, grasses, and several jumping cacti. A second set of tracks ran parallel to the first, about a dozen feet to the side, and this set of tracks led right over the top of some creosote bushes and cacti. Even from the car they could see that no effort had been made to minimize the damage. The bushes surrounding the hole were broken, and soil had been slung in every direction.

They got out of the car and walked along the tracks, looking down. "Here," Joe said, pointing at two footprints. "Whoever was directing the truck as it backed up was wearing cowboy boots."

Perez snorted. "That's a really useful clue. Out here half the population wears cowboy boots."

"We don't have a tape measure with us, do we?" Joe asked, ignoring Perez.

"As a matter of fact," Frank said, pulling a small tape from his pocket, "we do." He tossed it to Joe, who pulled out the end and measured the length of the clearest footprint.

"Twelve and a half inches," Joe said. "About a size twelve. I'm a size ten, so we can guess the guy was my height or bigger. Maybe six feet or more."

"We can't say for sure, but that sounds right," Frank said. "Come here and look at this." He pointed to the deep crosshatched pattern of the tire tracks and to a notch in one of the crosshatches. "See this notch?" he said. "Look, it appears here and again over here as the tire rolled along. Hand me the tape." He measured the distance from one notch to the next, and noted the measurement in a pocket notebook.

"What can you tell from measuring that?" Perez asked.

"By measuring the distance between notches, we can tell how big around the tire is. We can use this information to figure out the size of the tires," Frank said.

"But aren't big truck tires all pretty much the same size?" Perez asked.

Joe laughed. "I thought you said you noticed everything, Perez," he said, his voice slightly mocking. "Tires come in many sizes."

"But don't a lot of trucks have the same size tire?" Perez said.

"If we know the tire sizes," Frank said, "then at least we can tell when a truck is *not* the right one, because it won't have the right tires. And we can try to match the tread pattern."

"I get it," Perez said. He watched Frank and Joe pace the length of the two parallel crushed paths until they came to the large, uneven hole a few feet past the end of the tracks. About six feet across, the outer part of the hole was shallow, but the center was about four feet deep. The edges were littered with broken branches and footprints.

Joe pointed to the footprints around the hole. "One set of prints is cowboy boots," he said. "The other looks like sneakers or running shoes." He stooped down and measured the sneaker prints.

"It must have been a huge cactus," Perez said, "if they had to dig a hole that big to uproot it. How could they possibly have lifted something that big out of the ground?"

"With a crane," Frank said. "They dug all around the roots, loosened the soil, and then lifted the plant, roots and all, with a crane. That's the only way they could have done it, I think."

"I'll bet it weighed tons," Perez said. "A cactus is heavier than other plants because it holds so much water. The crane must have been very powerful."

Frank heard a vehicle approaching. He watched the road until he saw a gray motor home come around the bend and go on by, the driver scarcely glancing at the boys.

"Not much traffic out here, is there?" Joe said.

"Later in the morning there will be," Perez said. "People like to drive around this loop and check out the desert. But I don't think too many of them get up early in the morning."

"Before it gets too late, we'd better catch up with Kidwell," Frank said.

"Who's Kidwell?" Perez asked.

As they walked back to the car, Frank told Perez of Grish's suspicions about Kidwell. "We're supposed to keep an eye on him," Frank said. "Grish gave him a work assignment a few miles up the road."

"Does he know he's a suspect?" Perez asked.

"Nope," Joe said.

"You know," Frank said to Joe after they had gotten in and driven off down the road, "I've been thinking about that. Kidwell got awfully upset at Grish yesterday. And before that he almost ran us off the road. He may suspect that Grish is on to him."

"In which case we'd better be careful how we approach him," Joe said. "Working way out here, he can hear our car coming from a long way off. We don't want to be too obvious. How far is this place he's working?"

Frank pulled out the map. "Well, he's about here," he said, pointing to a spot on the map, "and I think we're about here." He scrutinized the map. "These lines show where the mountains are. It looks like there's a hill not far from the road just before we come to the place where he's supposed to be working. We could park the car and check out what he's doing from the top of the hill."

They drove for about ten minutes, with Frank checking the map. Finally he said, "I think this is our hill on the right. Pull over here."

Joe pulled the car over and parked. The three of them got out and hiked up a steep, brushy hill, bending low when they got to the top, where the bushes were less dense, so that Kidwell wouldn't see them on the crest. "This'll be our lookout point," Frank said.

Joe saw that the road continued around to the other side of the hill as it made a one-way fifty-mile loop through the western half of the park. Two hundred yards from the base of the hill he saw a scene similar to the one they had just visited—a swath of crushed vegetation leading from the road to a partly filled-in hole. There was no sign of either Kidwell or his truck.

"Maybe he's parked over there under those mesquite trees," Perez whispered, pointing to a copse of dull green trees. "I'm pretty good at moving around in the desert unnoticed—it helps me get pictures of animals. Why don't I go down there to see if he's around?"

Joe and Frank looked at each other and nodded. "Okay," Frank said, "but stay out of sight, and come right back."

Perez headed back down the way they had come. While Frank and Joe were waiting, they heard another vehicle coming slowly along the road. They waited for it to pass in view of their lookout. They couldn't see it, but it sounded as if it had come to a stop near where the Hardys had parked. After a few moments it sped up again, and when it came into view, Frank and Joe saw it was a yellow Volkswagen van, not Kidwell's truck. Disappointed, they waited, watching for a glimpse of Perez, but he never came into view among the many rock outcroppings and bushes.

After about fifteen minutes, Perez reappeared at the top of the hill with them. "I was right," he said. "Kidwell is parked under those mesquite trees, and he's sitting in his truck. He seems to be doing paperwork."

"Did you notice who was in that yellow van?" Joe asked.

"What yellow van?" Perez said. "I was sneaking up on Kidwell."

"You'll never make a great detective," Joe said, "until you notice everything around you."

"What's the big deal?" Perez said, his voice rising. "I said I was sneaking up—"

"Keep it down!" Frank whispered firmly. At that moment he heard an engine start up in the distance. He saw Kidwell's truck pull out onto the road from under the trees and drive away. The three jumped up and hurried down the hill before he could get too far ahead of them. It took them several minutes to get back to the car, and they were out of breath when they arrived.

Joe threw open the driver's door and then stopped. "I smell gasoline," he said.

Frank said, "I do, too." At the same moment he and Joe got down on their knees and looked under the car. There was a large wet spot underneath.

Joe reached over, touched the wet spot, and smelled his fingers. "Gas," he said.

Frank, easing his shoulders farther under the car, touched a rubber hose. "It's been cut!" he cried. "Somebody cut our fuel line."

7 The Secret in the Footprints

"It's been sliced right through," Joe said, peering under the car at the hose Frank was pointing out. "Unless we can figure out a way to splice it or bypass the cut, we either wait for someone to come along and give us a ride or we walk."

"But it's ten or fifteen miles back to the campground," Perez said.

"That shouldn't be a problem for an experienced desert rat like you," Frank said.

"Experience hasn't got anything to do with it," Perez said. "We're talking about a long walk, with no water or food."

Joe opened the trunk, looking for a piece of tubing he could use to splice the gas line. Finding nothing, he closed the lid. "Too bad this is a rental car," he said. "We carry extra tubing and belts in the van at home."

Cupping his hand above his eyes, Frank looked up and down the road. "Who do you suppose did this?" he asked.

Joe shook his head. "I don't see how it could have been Kidwell if he was sitting up there in his truck," he said. "It could have been whoever went by in the yellow van. Its driver could have stopped for a few moments."

"I don't remember seeing that van around the campground," Frank said. "Maybe it was Kidwell's accomplices. Perez, did you notice if Kidwell was talking on the CB radio?"

"His CB?" Perez shook his head. "He wasn't. He was sitting there doing paperwork."

"Why do you ask about the CB?" Joe said.

"It would explain how the people in the yellow van knew we were around," Frank said. "Kidwell could have been watching for us. He might have figured out that Grish would send us out to watch him. So he could have set it up so the yellow van went by at the exact right time to sabotage our car."

"Yeah, but we don't even know whether Kidwell realizes he's a suspect," Joe said. "One thing's for sure, though. Whoever did this knows about the cactus thefts in the park and knows what we're doing."

Joe peered under the car again. "There must be

62

some way to bypass this slice," he said as he scooted on his back under the car.

"You know what?" Frank said. "This wasn't necessary. Whoever did this—whether it was Kidwell or somebody in the yellow van—could have just left us alone and then gone ahead with their schemes when we weren't looking. Somebody wanted us to get a message."

Joe slid out from under the car. "Yeah," he said. "And the message is this: start walking or start hitchhiking. There's no way we're going to be able to repair the gas line without some extra tubing. Perez, you said traffic usually starts to pick up later in the morning?"

"That's right," Perez said. "But I don't know if it will actually pick up today."

"Well, you're a real font of information," Joe cracked.

"If we start walking now," Frank said, before Perez and Joe started going at it, "we should be back at the campground in about three hours. Before we get started, though, let's check out the place where Kidwell was working. Maybe we can pick up some clues to what he was up to."

In silence they walked the half-mile distance to the grove of mesquite trees where Perez had seen Kidwell. There were fresh tire prints on the shoulder of the sandy road, exactly where Perez had said he'd seen Kidwell parked. Just beyond the mesquite trees they found the destructive trail of the cactus thieves, and the pattern there was similar to

63

what they'd seen earlier: two sets of heavy tire tracks mutilating everything in their path, with a big hole at the end. This time the hole had been filled in, and there were scrape marks from a shovel all around it.

Perez squatted down and flicked his finger at a small white spot.

"What have you got, Perez?" Frank said.

"Nothing," Perez said. "I thought it was a cigarette butt, but it was just a little rock. Man," he added, waving his hand at the destruction, "this is really sick. Who would do something like this?"

"I wish I knew," Frank said. "But it looks as though Kidwell was only doing his job while he was here."

Joe nodded. "Okay, then, let's hit the trail. The road is a one-way loop. The shortest way back to the campground is against the direction of the loop. If we get a ride from someone, they'll be coming back around this way, so we'd get back in the same amount of time if we walked. I vote for walking back."

Perez groaned, but Frank agreed with Joe. They started back toward the road.

As they passed the place where Kidwell had parked, Joe veered off for a moment and said, "Go ahead. I'll just be a second." He poked around, looking at the ground.

"Man, is that guy always looking for clues?" Perez said.

"Only when he's investigating," Frank said. He

glanced back and saw Joe walking slowly, head down. He looked up at Frank and Perez, and then down again. Then, abruptly, he started jogging briskly toward them.

"What's up, Joe?" Frank asked.

"Oh, nothing," Joe said. "I was just checking to see if Kidwell did anything around his truck."

"And did he?" Frank asked.

"I . . . couldn't tell," Joe said.

Frank glanced at him curiously, wondering at his hesitation. "What do you mean you couldn't tell?" he asked.

"I mean I couldn't tell," Joe said. He gave his brother a look that said he didn't want to talk about it in front of Perez. The two brothers tried to hang back a little, but Perez slowed down to their pace as they walked along in the middle of the deserted road.

"Are you guys sure you want to walk?" Perez said. "Someone is bound to come along and give us a ride."

Neither Frank nor Joe answered him. They walked in silence for a while. Joe was thinking about an ice-cold lemonade, and Frank was wishing he had worn a hat to shield his head from the sun.

"Do you hear that?" Joe asked ten minutes into their journey.

"A truck," Frank said.

Perez grinned. "Enough exercise for today," he said. "I'm for getting back to the campground and solving this case."

Just then a pickup came over the rise, headed their way.

"Great," Perez said. "We can ride in the back, and nobody will complain if you get the upholstery dirty, Joe."

"I wouldn't get my hopes up," Frank said, watching the oncoming vehicle.

"Why not?" Perez said.

"That's Professor Townsend's truck," Joe said.

"Oh, no," Perez said. "Dr. Crabby."

"And we're not too popular with him right now," Joe said. He moved off the road, and Frank and Perez joined him. The truck drew closer, and Perez held up his thumb for a ride.

Townsend, with Diane beside him, slowed down and nearly came to a stop. Then he must have realized who the three hitchhikers were. He sped up and spat out the window as he went by.

The truck moved away, but a few moments later the red brake lights came on, and it slowed down.

"Maybe he's thinking it over," Perez said.

"Yeah, and maybe the sun is going to turn blue," Joe said. "Probably Diane is arguing with him. If it was up to Professor Townsend, he'd let us rot out here."

As they watched, the backup lights came on, and the truck began to back toward them.

"He's changed his mind," Frank said. "It must have been Diane's doing."

When the truck came abreast of them, Townsend scowled and said, "Are you three stranded?"

"Yes, sir, we are," Frank said. "We—"

"What happened to your vehicle?" Townsend demanded. "Is it broken down somewhere?"

"Yes, sir," Frank repeated. "As a matter of fact, it's a mile or so up that way. It appears that someone—"

"What's wrong with it?" Townsend said, interrupting again.

"Someone," Frank began, "or rather something happened to the fuel line. We have to go back for some tubing to fix it."

Townsend drew a deep breath and looked ahead into the distance. "Get in the back," he said. "All three of you. I've got some tubing that might be the right size, and some duct tape you can put around it if it's too big."

"Yes, sir," Frank said, waving to Joe and Perez to get into Townsend's truck. "The car is by the side of the road. You can't miss it. It's the tan Toyota."

"I know what it looks like," Townsend said. "Get in, though I don't know why I should help you, after all the damage you've done."

Frank went to the back and climbed in with Joe and Perez. They sat on the floor of the truck bed as Townsend started off down the road. The truck had metal shelves built along the front and sides, and the shelves were filled with transparent plastic boxes containing tools, spare parts, and various kinds of measuring instruments.

"Looks like a laboratory on wheels," Joe said. "I wonder what his project is all about."

67

"Well, if we ever get on speaking terms with him, we can ask," Frank said.

"That might be easier said than done," Joe said.

"Boy," Perez said, "isn't that the truth! He really doesn't like you guys, does he?"

"Nope," Joe said.

"What did you do, tell him he was a suspect or something?" Perez said. "Does he know about the cactus thefts?"

"We don't know," Frank said. He started to say more but felt a slight push from Joe's foot. At the look in Joe's eye, he shut up.

After a few minutes the truck slowed down and pulled off onto the shoulder of the road. Diane and her father walked around to the back as the Hardys and Perez piled out.

The professor asked, "What size tubing do you need?"

Joe said, "I'm not sure. This is a rental car, and we don't have any tools with us. Maybe half-inch tubing will do."

Townsend frowned for a moment, then said, "Don't think I have any. I've got a better idea."

He climbed into the truck as Diane asked, "Have you guys been walking long?"

"Not long," Frank said. "Maybe ten or fifteen minutes."

"It's a good thing this isn't July," she said. "It gets awfully hot out here in the summer."

"That's what we heard," Joe said. "We—"

Townsend came out with a roll of gray duct tape

and a small toolbox. "Here," he said, handing them to Joe. "See what you can do with that."

Joe took the tape and the toolbox and scrambled under the car.

"Let's go, Diane," Townsend said. "We've got work to do."

"Thanks a lot," Frank said.

"Don't mention it," Townsend said stiffly. "I'll get my tools back later in the day." He started off, then turned back. "And next time you think I'm doing something wrong, talk to me first, before you call in the rangers."

"I tried to, Professor," Frank said. "You wouldn't—"

"Aah!" Townsend exclaimed with a wave of his hand. "Never mind." He got into the truck, started it up, and as soon as Diane closed her door, drove off.

"Like I said—Dr. Crabby," Perez said. "What was he talking about—calling in the rangers?"

"Oh," Frank said, "last night we found—"

"Hey, Frank!" Joe called from beneath the car. "I need you to hold something."

Frank bent down. Joe scooted over to him and whispered, "Don't tell him anything. I'll explain later."

Frank straightened up and looked at Perez, wondering what was bothering Joe.

"Frank," Joe called again, "open up the hood. I need to poke this hose up toward the carburetor."

Frank did as Joe asked, and before long they'd

repaired the fuel line and were ready to get back on the road. As they piled into the car, with Joe at the wheel, he said, "I want to check out something at the spot where Kidwell was parked. It will just take a second."

He pulled the car around the bend to the grove of mesquite trees and got out, with Frank and Perez following him. "Perez, cross the road and stand over where the truck tracks start."

"Where the cactus thieves pulled their trucks off the road?" Perez asked.

"Yeah," Joe said. He watched as Perez walked across the road and down the shoulder. As soon as he was out of earshot, Joe said quietly to Frank, "Without making a big deal out of it, I want you to look at the footprints beside my right foot." He raised his voice and called, "That's the spot, Perez. Stand still for a second." Joe raised his arm and pointed toward Perez, as if he were showing Frank something.

In the meantime, Frank nodded and then glanced down at the footprints. "I see a set of prints that look as if they were made by sneakers," Frank said.

"Okay, Perez," Joe called, looking into the distance at Perez. "That's it."

Raymond trotted back as Joe walked Frank several feet in the direction Perez had come from.

"So what's up?" Perez asked, clearly puzzled as to what the Hardys were doing. "Did you figure something out? What's happening, guys?"

"Don't sweat it, Perez. We're just trying to get a better picture of things," Joe said. "We'd better get back to the office now." When Perez turned and headed toward the car, Joe pointed to Perez's footprints. They were identical to the footprints Joe and Frank had just studied.

"I get you," Frank said. "Instead of sneaking up on Kidwell, Perez came down the hill to talk to him. He walked right across the road. Kidwell couldn't possibly have missed him."

"Perez and Kidwell must be working together," Joe said, shaking his head in disgust. "And we're the ones who talked Grish into letting Kidwell's accomplice work with us."

8 Two Shakes of a Snake's Tail

Lost in thought, Frank and Joe got into the car. Joe took the wheel and, every now and then, cast a suspicious glance in the rearview mirror at Perez. I can't believe Frank and I were so easily taken in, Joe thought. That weasel! He wanted to give the guy a piece of his mind, but now wasn't the time. If Frank and Joe pretended to keep him in their confidence, maybe Perez would lead them to the rustlers.

Perez was in a talking mood. "Man," he said, "what a day! You guys sure do interesting things. I never had anyone cut my fuel line before. I'll be glad when we catch up to those people in the yellow van. What a hassle they caused us."

As Perez chattered on, Frank focused his thoughts on this new turn of events. If Kidwell was indeed involved in the cactus thefts, and if he and Perez were working together, then Perez was keeping track of the investigation. He could even be providing evidence to steer the investigation in the wrong direction. The Hardys would have to talk this over once they returned to the campground and got rid of Perez for a while.

"Hey!" Perez yelled. "There's Professor Townsend's truck. He must be doing his research somewhere around here. His research"—Perez lowered his voice—"or something else."

"Something else?" Joe asked. "Like what?" He pulled over and stopped behind Townsend's pickup.

"You know what I mean," Perez said. "Something like the cactus thefts."

"Oh, well, why don't you share with us what you know about the cactus thefts, Detective Perez?" Joe said sarcastically.

Frank opened his door to get out, then said, "Let's be careful how we discuss things where other people might overhear us, okay?" He glared at Joe.

"You got it," Perez said, getting out. "I wonder where they are."

There was no sign of either Professor Townsend or Diane. The mesquite and creosote were thick in this area, and half a dozen organ pipe and saguaro cacti grew within a hundred yards of the road. Townsend and his daughter could be anywhere in such a wild landscape.

"Too bad we can't climb up there," Perez said, pointing to a steep mountain that overlooked the area. "From that vantage point we could see anybody along the road for miles, but the soil on the mountainside is so crumbly you can't climb it directly. You'd have to go up the cliff face."

"Actually, we could," Joe said, "if we had some time. Frank and I are pretty good climbers. But I only stopped here to drop off Professor Townsend's tape."

"Joe," Frank said, "why don't you and I take a short hike back through the trees to see if we can spot the professor. Raymond, just in case they come back while we're gone, why don't you wait here? We won't go far."

Perez looked anxious at first but finally smiled and said, "Sure. If they show up, I'll give a yell."

"Good," Frank said. "We'll be back in no time." He glanced behind him at Perez, who was leaning on the car with his arms folded, then headed into the desert with Joe.

"So what are we going to do about this guy?" Joe asked. "If he's in cahoots with Kidwell, there must be some way we can make him give himself away."

"Yeah, but how?" Frank said. "Meanwhile, we still have some unanswered questions. What's the professor's connection to all this? I'm hoping we can find him and Diane out here so we can see what they're doing. It would be handy to rule them out as suspects so we could concentrate on Kidwell and Perez."

Joe held up a hand. "Look," he whispered. "Here comes Diane. She's headed back to the truck."

"Great," Frank said. "We can talk to her without her father around."

At that moment she spotted them, too, and started toward them. "Hi, guys," she said with a smile. She was wearing an orange day pack, which seemed to be full. "Looking for my dad?"

"Yeah," Joe said. "We were on our way back to the campground, and we saw your truck. Thought we'd return the tape."

She shook her head and removed her cap. "He's busy with his work, and he absolutely hates to be interrupted. You're already on his bad side, if you know what I mean. So if you really want to blow it, interrupting him would be a good way to do it. You can bring the tape back this evening at the campground. By the way, it's about time we officially met," she added. "I'm Diane."

Joe and Frank introduced themselves, and she began walking toward the road, motioning the Hardys to walk with her. "I'm just bringing out samples for him to run tests on later," she said.

"What exactly is he doing his research on?" Frank asked.

"He's investigating possible medicinal properties in cacti such as the organ pipe," she said.

"Is he always so hard to get along with?" Joe asked.

Diane bristled. "He works very hard, that's all,"

she said. "So do I. I'm a freshman at the university, and this is how I'm paying my expenses. I've been working as his assistant since last year, when I graduated from high school."

"Why did he get so mad when we found that piece of cactus under his truck?" Joe asked.

"I'm not sure," she said. "Maybe because in his line of work he can't afford to get a reputation for being careless about protecting the desert."

"That makes sense," Joe said.

As they walked around some tall bushes, the two vehicles came into view. Perez was standing exactly where he'd been before, only now he was wearing a broad smile and was nearly trembling with excitement.

"What's up, Perez?" Joe asked.

Perez's grin grew wider. "Just glad to see you guys, that's all," he said. After greeting Diane, he said to the Hardys, "I'm ready to head back if you are."

"Why the sudden hurry?" Joe asked.

"No reason, especially." As Perez spoke, he glanced significantly at Diane, as if he was trying to tell Joe something.

Joe opened the driver's door of the car. "Tell your father thanks," he said to Diane, "and we'll bring back the tape tonight."

Diane slid her pack off and opened the door of the pickup. "I'll tell him," she said. "See you there."

Frank and Perez got into the car. As Joe started it

up, Perez said, "I want you guys to look on the other side of the road, by that clump of dead grass. Don't let Diane see you looking. What do you see?"

"A pile of rocks," Joe said. The pile was four stones high, made with flat rocks stacked one on top of the other. "That's a common way for hikers to mark a trail. What about it?"

"Do you see any hikers around here?" Perez asked.

"What about it? What are you saying, Perez?"

"I'm saying that you're right," Perez said. "That's a marker. But you know what? I saw a marker like that at that first place we looked at this morning, the one I found for you."

Frank exchanged glances with Joe. This could be important, he thought. "So you think that marker might show where the thieves are going to hit next?" he asked.

"Maybe not where they'll hit next," Perez said, "but probably where they'll hit soon." He elbowed Joe lightly in the arm and said, "And you said I don't notice things, Joe. I'll bet you missed that marker this morning, didn't you?"

Joe nodded. "I did," he said flatly, pulling the car onto the road. As they passed the professor's pickup, Diane looked back and waved.

"There's more," Perez said. "While you guys were out walking, I took a good look in Professor Townsend's truck. Know what I found? A winch! A big one. A winch big enough to handle a good-size cactus."

"I didn't see a winch when we got a ride with him before," Frank said.

"That's because it's anchored at the front of the truck bed, not the back," Perez said, "and it has a cardboard box over it. Looks like a box of parts or tools. The winch is heavy-duty, with steel cable. If he ran the cable up and over a high frame, it could lift a pretty big cactus right out of the ground. Not a giant cactus, but certainly a small- to medium-size one." Perez folded his arms across his chest. "Personally, I think I just solved the case."

Neither of the Hardys said anything. They both knew Perez hadn't solved the case. If they assumed he wasn't one of the accomplices, he might have discovered some important clues. But they couldn't assume that. He might have made up the winch story to throw suspicion away from himself and onto the professor. Still, all the way back to the campground, they found themselves watching the sides of the road for little rock piles.

When they arrived at the campground, it was midafternoon. "I'm thirsty," Perez said. "You guys want some iced tea?"

"I think we'll just drop you off," Joe said. "I'm kind of curious about what our father's been doing all day."

"Okay," Perez said. "I'll catch up with you later."

Perez got out, and Joe drove to the Hardys' campsite. Fenton wasn't there. "Probably somewhere with Grish," Joe said. They drove to the

78

office, where they found Grish at his desk, talking to Fenton, as they'd expected.

Fenton was in a good mood. "We've been having a great time, catching up on the old days," he said. "I also ran a check of David Kidwell. It turns out that he may have been indirectly involved in cactus rustling up in Phoenix. Some of his workers used his company's equipment to steal some plants. Kidwell wasn't charged, but his company's reputation was destroyed, and he was ruined."

"I was right, wasn't I?" Grish said. "He sounds more and more like our boy."

"How about you guys?" Fenton asked. "Did you come up with anything?"

"Yeah," Joe said. "It's been quite a day." He and Frank related the events of the day to Fenton and Grish.

Grish took careful notes for his reports, and he seemed concerned to hear that someone had cut the Hardys' fuel line. "Why would anyone do such a thing?" he asked.

"My theory is they wanted to tell us there'd be trouble if we kept on investigating the case," Frank said.

"Do you really think so?" Grish said. "Maybe it was only pranksters or kids doing some vandalism."

"I doubt it," Joe said. "The timing was too coincidental with what we were doing, keeping an eye on Kidwell." He told Fenton and Grish about Perez's pretending to sneak up on Kidwell and instead meeting with him.

Grish's eyes grew wide at that. "You're kidding," he said, a smile beginning to form. "Do you think Raymond Perez might be one of Kidwell's accomplices?"

"We're not sure," Frank told him. "They seem to know each other, but we don't know what that means. There's another connection, though. Perez pointed out that the theft sites seem to be marked the same way hikers mark trails, with little piles of flat rocks."

Grish looked thoughtful. "That's true," he said. "I've got that somewhere in my notes, but I guess I forgot to mention it. What about it?"

"There was a marker like that at the spot where Professor Townsend was working today," Joe said.

"And?" Grish said.

"And," Joe continued, "that could mean there is going to be a theft there soon. And Townsend could be involved."

Grish's eyebrows shot upward. "Good work!" he exclaimed, smiling broadly. To Fenton he said, "These boys of yours are really something, aren't they?"

"The apples don't fall far from the tree," Fenton joked, and they all laughed.

Grish picked up a pencil and tapped it on his desk. "It's something to consider, about Townsend being involved," he said. "But I'm still thinking the real culprit is Kidwell, and now maybe Raymond Perez, too. I think that's where we should focus."

"There's a way to find out whether Townsend is

involved," Joe said. "How about if Frank and I stake out the area where he was working today? A good-size hill overlooks it, so we could keep an eye on a larger area. We can take our sleeping bags and climbing gear in case we need it."

"I don't like that idea, Joe," Grish said, frowning. "It's one thing to walk around in the desert during daylight hours, but it's another to be up on a mountain at night where help can't get to you quickly if you slip and fall. I'd hate to be responsible for something like that."

"But—" Joe said.

"The answer is no," Grish said firmly. "Remember that I'm in charge here. What I think you guys should do this evening is keep an eye on Perez to see if he and Kidwell get together again."

Joe looked to Frank and his father for help.

"Grish, I don't think you realize it," Frank said, "but Joe and I are very experienced outdoorsmen and climbers."

"I'm sure you are," Grish said. "But as I said, I'm concerned about your safety. That's part of my job as head ranger. If we can find a solid connection between Perez and Kidwell, we'll have solved our case."

"My own opinion," Fenton said, "is that my sons and I should get out of your hair and let you get some work done. We'll get something to eat and check back with you in a little while about the next step in the investigation. Don't you agree?" He gave Frank and Joe a stern, fatherly look.

They took their cue and stood up. "See you later, Grish," Joe said.

"Thanks, Fenton," Grish said with a smile. "And thanks for your help, guys. I really do appreciate it. Keep an eye on Perez, and see if anything happens between him and Kidwell. That's the best help you can give me."

Frank gave him a slight wave as he followed Fenton and Joe out the door. They got in the car and headed back to the campground.

"Dad," Joe said as he drove, "you think the stakeout is a good idea, don't you?"

"I'm not sure," Fenton said. "I don't think it's a bad idea, but we have some other strong leads as well. And Grish is probably right—there's some danger involved. Necessary danger is one thing, but I don't think this is necessary danger."

"Look at it this way, Dad," Frank said. "We need to know if Townsend is involved, right? The thefts have been occurring pretty frequently, so it seems likely the thieves will hit again tonight. If Townsend is involved, he may hit the place where he was working today."

"He must be home now," Joe said as he pulled into the Hardys' campsite and saw Townsend's truck in his site.

"Look at that!" Joe exclaimed. He pointed at the Hardys' motor home. The door was slightly open, and the edges of it were dented, as if someone had pried it open. "That door was fine a little while ago."

Joe got out of the car, walked cautiously toward the motor home, and climbed the steps. Gently he pulled at the door. As it came open, he heard a noise. A menacing, deadly noise that made his skin crawl. Joe swung the door open and froze when he saw what was inside.

9 Straight Up for Trouble

Gathering his wits, Joe shoved the door closed. "There's a rattlesnake in there!" he announced.

"What?" Fenton came over, eased the door open a crack, and peeked in. "You're right. It's coiled up about two feet inside the door, ready to strike. Worse luck, the broom is inside. Frank, ask around and see if you can borrow a broom—or anything with a long handle."

While Frank went in search of a broom, Joe eased the door all the way open, careful to stand at arm's length in case the snake struck. Beside the snake was a burlap sack. "It looks as if someone set a bag inside with the snake in it," he said. "They left the end of the bag open so the snake could crawl out."

Raymond Perez came around the corner of the

motor home. "Hey, Joe," he called out. "Hi, Mr. Hardy. What's up?"

Fenton held up a hand to stop him, and said, "We have a little problem here. You'd better stand back."

"What is—" Perez began. Just then the snake's rattle buzzed, and Perez's jaw dropped. He walked up to the steps and asked Joe in a low voice, "Do you have a broom or a mop, anything with a long handle?"

"Frank is looking for one," Joe said. "Stay away from the door."

"I've worked with snakes before," Perez said. "Why don't you—"

"Just butt out, Perez," Joe said, jumping down the steps. "We'll take care of it."

Frank came back with Diane, who was carrying a broom in one hand and a wooden spoon in the other. "Here you go, Joe," Frank said. "I caught Diane while she was cooking."

"I have a way with snakes," Perez said, grabbing the broom from Diane and ducking past Joe.

"Perez!" Joe yelled. "Don't be stupid."

Perez opened the door and grinned at the snake. "Hey, little fella," he said. "These big monster people got you scared?" He eased the business end of the broom over the snake until the straw touched the floor beyond it. Then he swept the snake toward the door. The snake shook its rattles furiously but did not strike as it slid across the floor.

"Everybody stand back," Perez said. With one quick sweep, he flicked the snake out the door and onto the ground. It recoiled, ready to strike, its tail emitting a mean-sounding buzz.

"What we need now," Perez said, "is something like a long soup spoon. Got one of those on you, anyone? Diane?"

Diane handed him a wooden spoon.

"Now, watch this," Perez said. In a voice like an announcer's, he boomed out, "Do not try this at home, ladies and gentlemen. This is being done by a trained professional!" He poked the broom at the snake. It struck at the straw, and he pushed it aside. Then Perez reached down and pressed the spoon against the back of the snake's head, pinning it to the ground. The snake's body writhed as it tried to get its head free from the spoon.

Perez grasped the snake behind the head and picked it up. The body coiled and writhed around his arm as he lifted it high.

"Say, Mr. Snake," Perez said playfully, turning the snake's face toward him, "nice fangs you got there. I hope you brush every day."

"Very funny," Joe said. He picked up the burlap sack and opened it. "Let's put him in here," he said, "while he's waiting for the dentist."

Perez dropped the snake into the sack. "Actually," he said, "that little guy is very dangerous. I know it seemed like I was playing around, but I've handled lots of snakes and I know what I'm doing.

I'm glad one of you didn't get bitten before you saw him."

"So are we," Fenton said. He picked up the wooden spoon and handed it and the broom to Diane.

"Yeah, Perez," Joe said. "Thanks for the lecture. By the way, you guys, whoever left the snake also left us a note." He reached inside the motor home and pulled out a large piece of paper with bright green lettering that read, "Hardys, get out!"

"Somebody's not a happy camper," Frank said.

Diane's chin dropped. "What? Do you mean somebody would . . . ? On purpose? I can't believe it."

"Neither can we," Fenton said, taking the sack from Perez. "I think we should let this little fellow go in the desert, but I want to report this incident to the office first." Tying a knot in the end of the sack, he said, "I'll be back in a few minutes." He got into the car and drove off.

"Who would put a rattlesnake in your RV?" Diane asked.

"Don't you know?" Perez said.

Diane's cheeks colored with anger. "Are you suggesting that I put it there?" she said.

"Not necessarily you," Perez said. "But your father doesn't exactly like Frank and Joe, does he?"

Diane's eyes grew wide. "I—I can't believe you would say something like that," she stammered. Then she turned and stormed off toward her trailer.

Perez grinned. "I guess I could have been more diplomatic," he said.

"Look," Joe said, "thanks for helping with the snake, but I think you'd better go."

"But I—" Perez began.

"We've had enough excitement for the moment," Joe continued. "Now we've got things to do."

"Like what?" Perez asked.

"Maybe you should take advantage of the sunset and snap some cactus photos in the pink light," Frank said. "We'll catch you in the morning."

Perez hesitated, his eyes on Frank.

Frank nodded and said, "We'll see you tomorrow, Perez."

Perez finally shrugged. "Have it your way," he said. "See if I help you out of any more snake predicaments. Actually, snakes aren't the most dangerous creatures in the desert. People are. Keep your ears open tonight. We may catch those cactus rustlers yet."

"Thanks for the advice," Joe said sarcastically. After Perez had gone, Joe continued. "Whoever is trying to interfere with us is messing with the wrong guys. I think we should stake out Kidwell, Townsend, Perez, those guys in the yellow van—everybody."

Frank laughed. "Calm down," he said. "There are only two of us, and it might be hard to do all those stakeouts at once. Besides, who are the guys in the yellow van?"

"You're right," Joe said. "I'm just spouting off. I'll tell you what, though. I think we should stake out you-know-who." He nodded toward Professor Townsend's trailer. "We could load up our gear as soon as Dad gets back and have him give us a ride to that spot where Townsend was working today. We can sit up on that high cliff and keep an eye on the whole area."

"And what happens," Frank said, "if we're perched up there and we witness the thieves in action?"

"We'll take the CB, of course," Joe said.

Frank thought it over. "Good idea," he said. "I'll get the gear together. You grab some food and the sleeping bags."

Frank carried the coiled climbing ropes from the motor home and laid them out on the ground. As he checked them over, he could hear the professor's angry voice from inside the Townsends' trailer. Frank remembered what Perez had said to Diane about her father being responsible for the snake incident. He promised himself he would apologize to her tomorrow. He could see Perez, a dozen camp spaces away, looking toward the Townsends' trailer as if he, too, could hear the professor's voice.

At that moment Professor Townsend banged open the door to his camper and stomped off toward the rest rooms.

Perez jogged over to Frank. When he saw the climbing gear and sleeping bags, he said, "Are you guys gonna do some climbing? I've done a lot of stuff, but I never learned to climb. Could you show me how? I won't be in the way."

"Another time, Perez," Frank said. "It's getting late, and we want to get out of here soon."

Diane popped her head out of the trailer. As soon as she saw Perez, she slammed the door shut.

Frank wondered if she had wanted to talk to him and Joe. "See you tomorrow, Perez," he said. "We couldn't possibly take an inexperienced climber on an evening climb. Too dangerous. Good night." Then he stepped into the motor home, where Joe was rummaging through the cupboards.

"There's nothing in here but a box of granola bars and some trail mix of nuts and raisins," Joe said. "Not fancy, but it'll keep our stomachs full."

"Perez wants to go with us," Frank said. "He wants to learn to climb."

Joe groaned. "Man, that guy is a real pest," he said. "Is he still out there?"

"I don't know. I think Diane wanted to come over and talk to us, but she stopped when she saw Perez," Frank said.

"You don't think she knows something about him, do you?" Joe asked.

"Either that or she didn't want him yelling at her," Frank said. "Check and see if she's out there now."

Joe looked out the door. Professor Townsend was bent over the climbing ropes. "Is there something we can do for you, Professor?" Joe asked.

Townsend straightened up, startled at first, then angry. "Yes, there is," he said. "I understand that you accused my daughter of putting a rattlesnake in your RV. Is that correct?"

"No, sir," Joe said carefully. "It's not. The other guy who was here said something to Diane, but I don't know what he meant by it."

"Understand one thing, young man," Townsend said. "We are scientists, my daughter and I, not pranksters. We have no desire to be mixed up in whatever mischief you are involved in. Have you got that straight?"

Just then Fenton pulled into the campsite, with Grish close behind in his official truck.

"Remember what I said," the professor growled. At that, he went back to his campsite, marching past Grish and Fenton without so much as a nod.

"What was that all about?" Fenton asked, climbing out of the car.

"Professor Townsend says he doesn't like accusations," Joe said vaguely. He was concerned that Grish had shown up. The ranger would undoubtedly want to know why they had the climbing equipment out, and Joe didn't want to waste precious time explaining.

"I wonder what he meant by that," Grish said. "Say, what are all these ropes and things? You aren't planning to do what I think you are, are you?"

Joe grinned nervously.

Grish lowered his voice. "Don't forget I'm in

91

charge of this investigation," he said, "and I do *not* want anybody getting hurt over some cactus thefts. Tell me what you're planning."

Joe gave in and told him, pointing out that a stakeout from a high spot, instead of from the desert floor, could turn up something. If he and Frank could get started soon, they would have time to climb to a good vantage point above the area where Townsend had been working.

"Hey, Joe," Frank called from inside the motor home. "Give me a hand in here for a sec."

Joe excused himself and went inside. Frank said quietly, "If we are going to do this thing, we'd better get moving."

Fenton came in to see what was going on. "Dad," Frank said, "you need to help us get out of here before dark. Otherwise this plan isn't going to work."

Fenton nodded, drew a breath, and went back outside, Frank and Joe behind him. "Listen, Grish," he said. "My sons are bright and experienced. They know what they're doing. I think I should just load them into the car, take them out where they need to go, and turn them loose. The worst that can happen is that they'll come home cold and tired in the morning."

Grish eyed both boys for a moment and then relented. "Be careful," he said with a sigh. "I don't want to be responsible if you get hurt."

"Don't worry," Frank said. He and Joe loaded

their gear into the trunk. "We'll be fine, just as my dad said."

As Frank was getting into the car, he saw Diane approaching their motor home. When she saw they were leaving, she turned abruptly and went back into her trailer. Frank looked at Joe. He'd noticed Diane's strange behavior, also, and could only shrug.

Fenton started the car and drove off while Frank fiddled with the walkie-talkie. "What channel should we use on the CB?" he asked. "How about channel five?"

Fenton shrugged. "You guys pick a channel, and I'll stay with it in the motor home."

"Channel five will work," Joe said. "Channel ten was the one we monitored last night when we picked up those voices. We can check channel ten and stay in touch on five."

"Channel five it is," Frank said, setting the dial on the walkie-talkie. "If we see anything suspicious, we'll call Dad, and he can notify Grish."

"I wonder what Diane wanted to tell us," Joe said.

"Whatever it was, she wanted to say it in privacy," Frank said.

Fifteen minutes later Fenton parked at the foot of the mountain. "Be careful," he said.

"No problem," Frank said.

"We'll be fine, Dad," Joe said.

Fenton waited while they slipped on their day

93

packs, which contained food, water, and extra sweaters. Then they slung the climbing gear over their shoulders and started toward the cliff.

"See you in the morning," Fenton called, and drove off.

Frank and Joe stopped and watched the taillights until they were out of sight. The desert suddenly seemed darker, bigger, and ominously silent to Frank.

"Let's move it," Joe said.

They walked to the cliff and looked up. "Piece of cake," Frank said. Joe nodded.

They put on their webbed climbing harnesses, which wrapped around their legs and waists. As they climbed, they would keep the ropes fastened to the harnesses. If one of them slipped or fell, the rope would catch him.

Joe went up first. Frank stood below, acting as belayer, letting out the rope gradually as Joe climbed up about six feet. At that point, Joe removed a wedge-shaped chock from his gear sling and wedged it into a fissure in the rock. He would use the chock to anchor his climbing rope to the cliff, to protect him in case of a fall. After placing the chock, he clipped the rope into a D-shaped silver ring called a carabiner, which was hanging from the chock, and continued upward. Every five or six feet, he placed another chock to anchor the rope.

Below him, standing on the ground, Frank kept the rope loose enough so that it didn't hold Joe back, but tight enough so that, if Joe did fall, he wouldn't fall far. Frank watched patiently as Joe worked his way up higher and higher, gripping the cracks and small outcroppings with his fingers and toes. From below, it was sometimes hard to see what Joe was hanging on to, but Frank knew that when his turn came, the grips would be obvious.

The sun was heading for the horizon in a hurry, he realized. They had less time before dark than they had anticipated. "I hope we don't run out of daylight," he called.

Resting his tired fingers for a moment as he stood on a small ledge, Joe looked at the setting sun, then at how much distance remained to the top. It looked like only about thirty feet. "I think we'll be okay," he called. "I should be at the top soon." He wedged another chock into a crack, clipped the rope to the carabiner, and continued upward.

When he finally reached the top, he tied the rope around a large boulder. "All set," he yelled down to Frank. "It's your turn."

Frank started up, bracing himself in the cracks and fissures, always moving upward. As he came to each of Joe's chocks, he jiggled it loose from the rock and clipped it to his gear sling. He knew he didn't need the chocks for protection, because Joe was holding the rope above him. When they came down in the morning, they would rappel from the top, swinging down, with the rope anchored to the top of the cliff.

The sun slipped below the horizon, and Frank climbed in the afterglow until he was halfway up. "When you get a chance," he yelled to Joe, "you'd better get the flashlight out. It'll be completely dark by the time I reach the top."

"Will do," Joe called back. "Be careful." He watched as Frank climbed higher and higher, and at a point where it looked as if he was balanced, Joe grabbed the flashlight from his pack and set it on the ground where he could reach it as he belayed the rope.

Frank did not stop to rest at the ledge, as Joe had, but pushed onward, trying to beat the oncoming darkness. His fingers were tiring, though. About ten feet from the top, he said, "Take the slack out. My fingers need a break."

Joe pulled the rope to create tension so that Frank could lean back in his sling, taking the pressure off his fingers for a minute or two.

"We need to work on our timing," Frank said as he rested his weight on the rope. "Next time let's—" Frank stopped in midsentence, his mouth gaping as the realization hit him.

Without warning, the rope had broken. With no time to react, Frank fell backward off the cliff and into the darkness.

10 The Jaws of Danger

"Frank!" Joe shouted frantically as he peered over the ledge. "Frank? Frank?"

"Don't worry, Joe," came Frank's voice hoarsely. "I've caught a ledge."

"Are you all right?"

"I think so. Just give me a minute," Frank called, trying to catch his breath. A small bush growing on the ledge had stopped Frank's downward plunge. He climbed out of it and leaned against the wall, clinging gratefully to its solidity.

Joe sat up straight, waiting and listening to the wind that was coming up with the setting of the sun. "Frank?" he called again, worried about his brother's safety against the windy rock face.

"I'm up on the ledge," Frank called back, "and

it's wide enough for me to stay here for the night. It's too dark to keep going. I'm strapping myself in with my sleeping bag around me. I'll be okay."

"Can I do anything for you?" Joe asked.

"Yeah, give me a wake-up call around seven," Frank answered.

Joe let out his breath and smiled with relief. He knew Frank was safe by the sound of his voice and the attempt at a joke. He took out the walkie-talkie, set it to channel 5, and pressed the transmission button. "Break five," he said.

There was no answer, so he tried again. "Break five. Dad, are you listening?"

Still no answer. The sun was gone, but there was a trace of light left. He decided to try again when it was completely dark, when there'd be less radio interference from the sun. Maybe the walkie-talkie wasn't strong enough to get a transmission all the way back to the campground in the daylight.

Except for the wind, the night was quiet, and the air grew increasingly chilly. Joe decided to keep warm and crawled into his sleeping bag. He munched on a granola bar while he listened to the CB. He wondered whether Frank had any food with him. Every now and then, out of the corner of his eye, he caught a glimpse of something flying through the air. He knew there weren't any birds flying around at night, except maybe owls, but the rustling sounds he heard sounded as if they came from something smaller. It must be bats, he decided.

"Frank?" he called out. "Do you hear the bats? Can you see them?"

"Yeah, I hear them," Frank called back. "No, I can't see them."

"Don't go getting yourself bitten," Joe said. "I'd hate to have to drive all the way to Phoenix at night because you've become a vampire and can't travel in the daytime."

"I'll try not to," Frank called. "Anything on the radio?"

"Not yet," Joe answered. He put out another call for his father on channel 5, but again there was no answer.

"Nothing on the CB," Joe called down to Frank. "I'll try again later."

"Okay," Frank answered. "In the meantime, I think you should scan the other channels."

"Roger," Joe called. "I'll do that. It'll help keep me awake." He switched from channel to channel, listening, but could pick up nothing more than static. He listened for a while on channel 10, where he and Frank had heard the voices the night before.

Just as he was about to switch back to channel 5 to try Fenton once more, a voice cut in, and he heard the words "boy detectives."

Joe almost dropped the walkie-talkie. He froze, listening for more. After a few moments the voice came back with "enjoy that wild-goose chase."

"Get off the radio," another male voice crackled. The voice sounded familiar to Joe, but it was so faint and the crackling so bad he couldn't place it.

He listened for a while longer, but there were no more transmissions.

"Joe, was that the radio?" Frank's voice rose up the cliff like a whisper. "Did you reach Dad?"

"No," Joe called back, "but I heard someone talking about us on channel ten. He called us boy detectives."

"Boy detectives?" Frank asked.

"Yeah, and they said something about a wild-goose chase," Joe called.

Frank was silent for a few moments. Then he called up, "I get the feeling we aren't going to see the cactus thieves tonight. How about you?"

"I have the same feeling," Joe answered.

After that, the two fell silent. Every so often, Joe tried to raise Fenton on the CB, but got no answer. He knew Fenton would be listening, which meant the problem was probably in the CB itself.

He lay awake, trying to figure out whom he'd heard on the CB. Joe recalled how he and Frank had left Perez alone while they'd gone looking for Townsend. Could Perez have built the stack of rocks himself to throw the Hardys off track? And what about the rope? Why had it snapped?

He listened to the coyotes howling in the distance, some behind him in the mountains, others out in the flat country. Coyotes out hunting in the darkness, just as he and Frank were hunting.

Joe moved over to the edge of the cliff and called down softly, "Frank, are you awake?"

"Of course I'm awake," Frank said. "This is a stakeout, don't you remember?"

Joe laughed. "Yeah, I remember," he said. "Listen, who thought of the stakeout up here?"

"It was you," Frank said. "You suggested it when we were talking to Grish. But Perez is the one who gave us the idea that something might be going on out here. He's the one who found the trail marker by Townsend's truck."

"That's what I was thinking," Joe said. "I wonder what Perez is up to tonight."

"So do I," Frank replied. "So do I."

They fell silent again, each looking out into the darkness.

The next thing Joe knew, Frank was pulling at the foot of his sleeping bag, trying to wake him up. Sleepily, Joe jerked his foot away and mumbled, "What time is it?" He pulled up the sleeping bag over his face and tried to go back to sleep.

Then he remembered Frank was stuck on a ledge partway down the cliff. How had he gotten up in the darkness? Joe yanked the sleeping bag down to say something to Frank—and found himself staring into the icy eyes of a coyote.

11 Not All Cowboys Are Heroes

Joe froze. Then he realized the coyote looked as startled as he felt. The coyote backed up a few steps and then dashed away. Joe started to laugh, then stopped. Up close, the coyote at first looked like a neighbor's dog. But it was a wild creature, its eyes fierce with wily intelligence.

The morning light was gray, as dawn was just beginning to light the sky. The silvery blue sky threw an odd light on the desert. The rocks, the plants, and even the mountains themselves looked like images on a video screen, not quite real. Joe climbed out of his sleeping bag and into the cold morning air.

"Guess what?" he yelled to Frank. "I just met a coyote." He walked to the edge and looked down.

About thirty feet below, Frank waved his end of

the rope. "Well," he called up, "this shouldn't come as a surprise to you. The rope's been cut. We've been sabotaged again."

Joe pulled up the rope and examined it. The end had been cut a little more than halfway through. He checked the rest of the rope, and then dropped a length to Frank, who quickly climbed to the top.

As they anchored the rope and prepared to rappel down, they saw the tan Toyota coming along the road.

"I'll bet Dad was worried about us," Frank said. "You never did raise him on the CB, did you?"

"Nope," Joe said, glad to see Fenton coming after them so early. He looped the belt through his harness and let himself carefully over the edge of the cliff. Then, leaning back against the rope and walking slowly down the face of the cliff, he rappelled to the bottom. Frank came after him. They coiled up the rope and then jogged out to the road, where Fenton stood by the car waiting for them.

Not until they were in the warm car did they realize how chilled they'd been in the cold desert air. As they sipped the hot cocoa Fenton had brought for them in a thermos, they told him about the events of the night. He had been listening on the CB but hadn't picked up any of Joe's transmissions.

"In fact," he said as he drove, "all I could pick up was static. I didn't even hear the transmissions you heard. Finally, about four o'clock in the morning, I went out with a flashlight to check the antenna. It was broken off."

"I wondered what was wrong," Joe said.

"Did you figure out whose voice you heard on the CB?" Frank asked him.

"No, but I hope to," Joe said. "Maybe I'll recognize it if I hear it again."

"Maybe it was the person who cut the rope," Frank said, "and who broke off the antenna on the motor home."

"Well," Joe said, "we know Raymond Perez could have cut the rope when we went into the camper to pack," Joe said.

"But he didn't have a knife," Frank said.

"Not that I saw," Joe said. "And Professor Townsend was also near the ropes. Grish was there, too, but he doesn't count," Joe said.

When they pulled into the campground, Grish was waiting for them at their campsite, standing beside his official truck. He grew angry when they told him someone had cut the climbing rope.

"That does it," he said. "You guys are off this case. I don't want anyone getting hurt, especially over some cacti. They aren't worth the risk. I'm going back to the office to call the state agricultural investigators. No offense, Fenton, but I'm beginning to think it would be a good idea if you guys just packed up and went back to Bayport."

Fenton nodded. "I'll stop by the office in a little while and we'll talk."

Grish hesitated as he was getting into his truck,

then said, "Seriously, Frank and Joe, this is getting too involved and dangerous. I want you to back off. Do I make myself clear?"

"Loud and clear," Joe said.

"Good," Grish said. "See you at the office, Fenton." He got into the truck and drove off.

"Well?" Fenton said. "What do you boys think?"

"You know what we think, Dad," Frank said. "How can we give up in the middle of a case? How can we . . ." He hesitated, distracted by the sight of Professor Townsend sitting in his pickup, trying to get it started. "You need some help, Professor?" Frank called.

Townsend didn't respond, perhaps because he couldn't hear inside the truck with the window rolled up. With Diane in the seat beside him, he was trying to start the engine, but it wouldn't quite catch.

"Sounds like he's out of gas," Joe said. "I think we should give him a hand, don't you?"

"Absolutely," Frank said.

They walked over together. Townsend rolled down his window, looking flustered and not at all happy to see them.

"Can we help?" Joe asked. "Is your gas gauge working?"

"Of course it's working," Townsend said with a snarl. "There should be plenty of gas."

"But it isn't getting to the carburetor," Joe said. "If you'll pop open the hood, I'll take a look."

Eventually they realized that the problem was a clogged fuel filter. "It's simple to fix," Joe said, "if we find a replacement."

After talking things over, they decided Joe would drive Diane and Fenton into Ajo, the nearest town, to pick up a filter. Fenton wanted to stock up on groceries, and so did Diane. Frank planned to put away the camping and climbing gear and maybe take a short nap after his cold night perched on the cliff.

"And," Frank added as they talked over their plans, "I should have a little talk with Perez. I want to see his paintings, to see if he's for real."

"Good idea," Joe said.

"What'll you do if you see something that links him to Kidwell?" Fenton asked.

"If Perez and Kidwell are partners in crime," Frank said, "they're smart enough not to let me see anything in the camper that would incriminate them."

"So you don't expect to get in?" Fenton asked.

"Not if there's anything in there that points to the thefts," Frank said.

"What are you guys talking about?" Diane asked, standing by the door of her father's truck. "What is this crime you're discussing?"

Frank looked at her, then at Joe. "It's a long story," he said. "You'd better get on the road, Joe. We've got things to do."

"You bet," he said. "Diane?"

With a quizzical look, Diane got into the front seat, and Joe climbed into the driver's seat. Fenton got in back, and they drove away.

Frank walked over to Perez's camper. Perez met him at the door. "So," Perez said, "how was your climb?"

"Funny you should ask," Frank said.

"You mean it was eventful? Did you spot the cactus rustlers?" Perez asked.

"I'll tell you what," Frank said. "You show me your paintings and I'll bring you up to date on our adventure."

"What?" Perez said. "Why do you want to see my paintings?" When he saw that Frank was serious, he licked his lips and glanced inside the camper. He wasn't his usual cocky self, Frank noticed.

"What can I say?" Perez said. "No one else has ever shown any interest, and . . . well, okay." He stepped back and waved Frank in.

Frank looked at the groups of three and four paintings stacked together, leaning against the walls, on the kitchenette table, even hanging from open cupboard doors. The paintings were of desert sunsets, mountains, cacti, and shrubs.

"So these are your paintings?" Frank said at last.

Perez chewed his lower lip and nodded. Frank looked at the painting on the top of each stack and leafed through the most prominent stack closest to the door. Some were on canvas. Others were on

107

wood. Propped up by the sink was a large dinner plate painted with a scene of a cactus garden. Frank let his eyes casually glance over everything in the trailer but could see nothing that tied Perez in with Kidwell or the thefts.

"There sure are a lot of paintings," he said finally.

"I know. I know," Perez said. "Actually, I'm supposed to be in art school at the university in Tucson, but I ran out of money. A friend lent me this old camper and I moved here. This is the cheapest place I could live until I can go back to school."

"Couldn't you get a job?" Frank asked.

"I looked, but I couldn't find anything," Perez said. "I figured an artist starving in the desert was more romantic than an artist starving in the city."

"They're not bad," Frank said, waving his hand at the paintings around him. "I like them." Obviously Perez was an artist, but Frank still couldn't get a sense of whether he was involved with the cactus thieves. A starving artist might stoop to stealing plants from a national preserve.

"Thanks," Perez said. "Do you want to talk some more? You still have to tell me about last night."

"Sure," Frank said, "but first tell me how you met David Kidwell."

"What?" Perez asked.

He seemed to have been caught off guard, so Frank pushed the point. "I said, tell me how you met David Kidwell. You two are obviously old friends."

"Oh, I don't remember exactly," Perez said. He hesitated for a moment, then added, "We just got to talking one day when he was working around the campground."

"What were you two doing yesterday when you went down the hill?" Frank said. "What did you tell him?"

"Nothing," Perez said. "I was just taking a look, like I said."

"Don't give me that, Perez," Frank said. "I know you and Kidwell had a talk."

"How did you . . . ?" Perez said. "Man, you guys are good. Okay, here's what happened. Kidwell and I got to be friends from just hanging out around the park. He's a hard guy to know because he's so quiet. When I overheard you and Joe talking the other day, I went to Kidwell and told him he was a suspect. Yesterday, when you were trying to spy on him, I went down the hill and told him. And while you and Joe were out looking for the professor, I put up that little rock pile to throw you off and make you suspect Townsend."

"Why'd you do that?" Frank said, opening the door.

"'Cause I knew Kidwell was innocent, and I wanted to keep him out of trouble. He's a loner, like me, and we've got to watch out for each other."

"Perez, I can't believe what I'm hearing," Frank

said. "If Grish finds out that you've discussed the case with Kidwell, that'll be the end of me. Now, listen, we're officially off the case under orders from Grish. So don't breathe a word to anyone about this investigation. Enough damage has been done already."

Frank sighed in frustration. No wonder Grish was so adamant about secrecy, he thought. There are wily coyotes all over this desert.

Meanwhile, halfway to Ajo, Joe apologized to Diane for the way Perez had accused her father of being responsible for the rattlesnake.

"I know Perez was being a jerk and not you guys," she said. "You and Frank are both very sweet." Without looking in his rearview mirror, Joe knew his father was grinning in the seat behind him.

"My father's been working very hard," Diane said. "My mother has a rare form of arthritis and is in a nursing home, which is very expensive. I'm used to Dad, but I always feel sorry for people who don't know him and don't know why he's like that."

"It's okay," Joe said, resisting the impulse to say that he and Frank were used to dealing with jerks.

Just outside of town they found an auto parts store and purchased a filter for the professor's truck.

Back in the car, Diane said, "I'm still waiting to hear your long story, Joe. What thieves were you talking about? Does it have something to do with the rattlesnake in your RV?"

Joe tried to think of something to say. Diane seemed innocent, but he and Frank had seen a lot of innocent faces on people who later turned out to be guilty. He decided to take an indirect approach. "Listen," he said. "You didn't happen to see anyone around our campsite yesterday afternoon, did you?"

"I was trying to tell you yesterday, when Perez interrupted, that I saw a tall, lean man wearing a cowboy hat hanging around your campsite just before you got back. He could have been the one who put the rattler in there. He'd have to be really knowledgeable about the desert, though."

"Why do you say that?" Fenton asked.

"Only a real desert rat would know how to find a rattler in January," Diane said. "They hibernate."

"Well," Joe said, "unless you can spot him again, you've given us a description that could fit a lot of men around here. Just take a look."

They were on the main street of Ajo, heading toward a rectangular plaza with shops around it. Adults strolled across the brown grass lawn and children played there. All the men wore blue jeans, even the ones in business jackets. Many were Native Americans. Most of the men wore cowboy hats. And any man who wasn't wearing a cowboy hat wore a baseball cap.

"That guy getting into the Jeep fits the description you just gave us," Joe said. "So does that guy crossing the street, and even that guy going into the restaurant."

"Why would anyone put a rattlesnake in your motor home, anyway?" Diane asked. "It just doesn't— Oh!" she cried out, and pointed. "Joe! That's him, right there!"

12 A Prisoner Is Taken

"That's him, I swear!" Diane cried, pointing.

"Which one?" Joe asked.

"Going into the café on the other side of the plaza," Diane said. "The one holding his hat in his hand and smoothing back his hair."

Joe stifled the impulse to floor the car and race around the plaza. He knew that the man might duck away if he was aware that someone was after him. Instead Joe pulled the car into a parking place near the restaurant.

"Are you going to confront him?" Diane asked.

"Oh, no," Fenton said. "Nothing like that. For now we're just curious. We don't want to get the guy stirred up so he runs."

"How about a soft drink?" Joe asked Diane as they all got out of the car. "In that café."

"Sure," Diane answered. "Are we going to follow him?"

"At a distance," Joe said. "If he's the one who put the snake in our motor home, he might recognize us. We have to be careful."

Once inside the café, they spotted the cowboy Diane had identified, sitting near the rest rooms in the back with another man, who was wearing a plaid shirt.

"Are you still sure it's him?" Joe asked.

"Yes. Remember, I'm a scientist-in-training," Diane answered. "I have an excellent visual memory."

"You two find a booth so they can't see you," Fenton said. "Order a coffee for me. I've got an idea." With a nod to Joe, he left. About ten minutes later he came back, carrying a denim jacket and a cap.

"Put these on, Joe," he said. "You need a disguise."

Seeing that the cap was too large, Joe started to adjust the tabs in back. But Fenton stopped him. "Pull it down low," he said.

When Joe was ready, Fenton said, "You can't see it from your side of the table, but there's a telephone alcove by the rest rooms. It's right by their table. Go back there and pretend to make a phone call. Listen to what they're saying, if you can."

"Be careful, Joe," Diane said.

"No problem," Joe said as he got up. Keeping his face turned away from the cowboy and the man in the plaid shirt, he walked back to the telephone, dropped in a quarter, and pretended to make a phone call.

The men weren't talking much. They seemed more interested in wolfing down their hamburgers.

"We got it on the map?" the cowboy asked. The other man's reply was indistinct. But after a few moments Joe heard the cowboy say, "So tonight is the last one? I thought we were gonna do a few more."

"We were," the man in the plaid shirt said. "But the boss says those pesky kids are getting in the way. This one's the last."

They talked some more, but Joe couldn't hear what they were saying.

Then he heard the man in the plaid shirt say, "You ready, Slim?"

"Yeah," the cowboy said, standing up. "Let's get out of here."

As they ambled to the register, Joe got his first good look at them. He recognized Slim, the cowboy, as the man they had seen in Grish's office the day before. The man in the plaid shirt was shorter and stockier, with long dark hair. So, according to Diane, Slim had been hanging around the campground, Joe mused. Perhaps Diane was right, and Slim was the one who'd planted the rattlesnake in their motor home.

After the two men left, Joe returned to the booth in time to see his father put a few bills on the table.

Fenton handed him a burger and said, "Sorry, son. You'll have to eat it on the way."

Joe shrugged at Diane as she slid out of the booth. He took a big bite of the burger and, with his mouth full, said, "Oh, well, that's the life of a detective."

When they got outside, they saw the two men climb into a pickup truck and drive off.

"Hey, that's Kidwell's truck," Joe said. "I saw it parked at Grish's office."

"Let's go," Fenton said, heading for the car, Joe and Diane hustling behind him.

"What did you hear inside?" Fenton asked as Joe started the car.

"Those two were talking about doing their last job tonight. And the cowboy's name is Slim," Joe added, pulling into traffic.

"Did they say why this was going to be their last job?" Fenton asked.

Joe grinned. "Yeah," he said. "They said something about some pesky kids getting too close."

"I see," Fenton said. "Well, pesky kid, let's not let those guys get too far ahead of us."

They continued a few blocks through town, following Kidwell's truck until it turned in to a motel parking lot and stopped next to a yellow van.

"Hey!" Joe exclaimed. "That's the yellow van that drove by when our fuel line was cut."

"You didn't tell me your fuel line was cut," Diane said. "You just said it was broken."

Joe didn't answer. He was watching the men enter a small bungalow unit.

"How did those guys know where to find us to cut the fuel line?" Joe asked. "Perez was with us, and I never saw Kidwell until we got to the site. Neither one of them could have radioed for these guys to come and cut our line unless the guys were waiting to do something like that all along."

"Joe, look at that semi," Fenton said pointing. Across the parking lot, among the cars, was a tractor-trailer truck. A few spaces away was a heavy-duty flatbed truck with dual rear tires. On the back of the flatbed was a large winch.

"Dad," Joe said, "I think we've found the thieves! This stuff could nail them red-handed."

"What are you talking about?" Diane asked.

Joe briefly told her about the cactus rustlers, and she looked shocked. "I didn't know anything about this," she said, "and I've been here for weeks."

"The head ranger has been keeping the investigation under wraps because of regulations," Fenton said. "And we need to check out a few things before we can point fingers. Please don't discuss this with anyone."

"That's true," Joe said. "Dad, I'm going to park down the street. I think we can check out these trucks without being noticed from the motel. Diane, why don't you wait in the car?"

"I'd rather come along," she said.

Joe didn't argue. He drove down the street and

parked, and the three of them sauntered back to the parking lot.

Approaching the flatbed truck, Joe reached into his back pocket and pulled out the pad on which he'd written the tire dimensions. Then, producing a measuring tape, he knelt to check the size of the truck's tires. "We've got a match," he said.

Fenton nodded, keeping an eye on the bungalow door.

The semitrailer's tires also matched the dimensions he and Frank had jotted down.

"I think we should take a peek inside the semi," Fenton said.

Joe glanced toward the bungalow. "I guess it's now or never. I hope the door doesn't squeak."

"Do you think we might find an organ pipe cactus?" Diane asked.

"Maybe," Joe said. He unlatched the rear door and pulled it partly open. He made out the shape of a large organ pipe cactus lying on its side with the arms pointing toward the door. It had a wooden frame around it.

"They seem to know what they're doing," Fenton said.

Joe nodded and said, "I wonder how many cacti are in there." He swung up into the dark trailer, with Fenton close behind him. They walked toward the front, slipping along the side beside the big cactus. Farther into the semi, they could see two more plants, both of them in wood frames.

"Let's go, Joe," Fenton said. "We can call the police from a pay phone— Wait," he added, slipping by Joe. He pulled out a handkerchief, then reached down and used it to grab something tucked below the cactus. It was a shovel. "There'll be fingerprints on this thing."

Joe jumped down, but Fenton stopped to examine the shovel in the sunlight. "Well, look at this," he said. He bent and held it out for Joe and Diane to see. Carved into the metal shank of the shovel was the name David Kidwell.

"So Grish was right," Joe said.

They heard voices. Joe looked up at his father. Someone had slammed a bungalow door, and the voices were headed their way.

"Let's get out of here," Joe whispered. He grabbed Diane and ducked behind the car next to the trailer just as Slim and the man in the plaid shirt came around the back of the trailer. There hadn't been time for Fenton to jump out. He sneaked back into the darkness.

Slim was saying, "I'll drive this rig, and you take the flatbed. . . . Look at this. You can't even close the door right. Did you get the shovel stowed in? You better have. I'm tired of you forgetting things."

Oh, no, Joe thought, a lump in his throat. They'll find Dad if they look for the shovel. He got ready to jump Slim, who had his hand on the door, if the man made a move to climb inside.

"Who made you the boss?" the man in the plaid

shirt shouted angrily from the front of the flatbed. "I remembered the shovel. It's in there by the cactus. I'm going to start this thing up now."

"Okay, okay," Slim said. "Don't get all riled up. I'll check the tires." As his partner started up the flatbed's engine, Slim latched the semi's door and slammed the bolt. Joe wanted to shout something out, but all he could do was grit his teeth and pound his fists on his knees. His father was trapped inside the trailer.

13 A Father
Goes Down

Joe's heart sank. He thought quickly. "Hang on," he whispered to Diane. "As soon as the truck starts to move, I'll get to the back of the trailer and unlatch the door. The driver has to back up before he can pull the rig out of the parking lot."

"Are those the rustlers?" she whispered.

He waved off her question and waited for his chance. But instead of backing out, the semi pulled forward in a wide arc, narrowly missing the cars parked in front of the bungalows. It headed out onto the street and away. Right behind it went the flatbed.

As soon as the trucks were out of sight, Joe grabbed Diane's hand and dashed for the car. They got in, he started the engine, and they sped through town, heading for the highway toward Organ Pipe. Once out on the highway, Joe pushed the speedometer up to the limit.

The trucks were nowhere to be seen. Joe knew they couldn't have gotten too far ahead of him. He should have caught up with them easily. "They must have taken another route," Joe said. He slowed down enough to make a U-turn and raced back to town.

Heading for the south end of town, Joe said, "Organ Pipe is off to the southeast, so they must have come in this direction." He drove through the dusty residential streets, looking for a road that led out of town. His stomach tightened into a knot as he thought about the trucks, with his father inside one of them, getting farther away with every second.

"You know what we need?" Joe said to Diane. "We need Frank and a good map. There must be a back road through here that goes to the park. Where else could the trucks have gone?"

He turned the car around again and sped back to the highway. In the twenty-minute drive back to Organ Pipe, his mind raced ahead, going over clues. The two men in the trucks were obviously working with someone who knew what he and Frank were up to. But who was it? Professor Townsend was out of the picture—Diane genuinely seemed to know nothing about the case, and if the professor were involved, Diane would be, too. He wondered how Frank's talk with Perez had gone. Almost certainly Kidwell was one of the crooks.

They were using his pickup, and his shovel was in the trailer with the cacti. Since Perez had some kind of connection with Kidwell, that meant that Perez was probably involved, too.

Joe knew that he and Frank would have to work quickly to get their father out of danger. He hoped Grish would be able to suggest some kind of back route the trucks could have taken from town.

Diane interrupted his thoughts. "Joe, are we going to call the police when we reach the park? Don't you think they could help?"

"Maybe," Joe said. "We'll call them from Grish's office."

"I got the license plate numbers of the trucks," Diane said.

"Terrific!" Joe said. "I was so worried about my father, I didn't think of it. Maybe the thieves won't open the door until they've dug up another cactus. That could be hours from now, which buys us some time."

"And it will be dark in less than an hour," Diane said. "That means your father can hide in a corner of the trailer until he has a chance to get away."

"That's true," Joe said. "In the meantime, we need to find them."

They were approaching the park office and the turnoff for the campground. As they passed the office, Joe noted that Grish's truck was parked by the building. He decided to go straight to the campground to find Frank.

As Joe pulled to a stop, tires squealing, Frank

came out of the motor home. "What's wrong?" he asked.

"They've got Dad," Joe said. He and Diane got out of the car. Diane went straight to her father's trailer while Joe explained the situation to Frank, including finding the shovel.

"We need that topo map," Joe said, "the one Grish gave us. I lost the trucks in town and I think they took an alternate route into the park."

Frank went inside for the map, and Diane returned with her father.

"What's going on here?" Townsend asked, his face showing genuine concern. "Diane tells me your father may have been kidnapped by a gang of thieves."

"Not exactly kidnapped," Joe said. "But he's trapped inside their truck."

Frank came out with the map, and they spread it on the picnic table. Joe gave Townsend a brief rundown of what had happened during the afternoon.

"Do you know of any way to get to the park from Ajo other than along the highway?" Joe asked Townsend.

Pointing at the map, Townsend said, "The town of Ajo is up this way. As you can see, there are no alternate routes into the park from that direction, unless the thieves have created their own road. I've driven and hiked all over that area."

"Then where could they have gone?" Diane

asked. "One minute they were ahead of us, then they were gone."

"I wonder if they could simply have gone to a different place in town," Frank said.

Joe thought about it and nodded. "That may be," he said. "But where? Professor, can you think of any place they would have gone?"

"I have no idea," Townsend said with a shrug. "Maybe they stopped for gas."

"Gas! That's it." Joe said. "Is there a gas station that isn't on the main route into town?"

"There are a couple," Townsend said. "You could easily have missed them."

"Then they could have gotten gas," Frank said, "and either returned to the motel or headed for the park."

"So they could be anywhere," Joe said.

"We should notify the police," Townsend said firmly. "And I suggest we do it immediately. These men are obviously dangerous."

Frank realized that he and Joe were going to have to move fast. Townsend could slow them down. "Professor," he said, "I think calling the police would be a good job for you. They'll take you seriously once they find out who you are. Why don't you go up to the office and ask Grish to call for you."

Joe caught on immediately. "Yes, Professor," he said, "the police will respond faster if the call comes from you."

"I'll help you replace that fuel filter right now, Professor," Frank said.

Townsend nodded. "Diane, coming along?"

She looked first at Joe, then at Frank. "No," she said. "I'll go with Frank and Joe."

"We'll catch up with you at the office, Professor," Joe said. "We have to let Grish know what's happening."

"All right, then, I'll see you all at the office," Townsend said, starting for his truck with Frank.

After Frank had fixed Townsend's truck and returned to the campsite, Joe said, "Frank, what did you find out about Perez? It's pretty obvious that Kidwell is involved."

Frank grinned. "You won't believe what I learned about Perez," he said. "First of all, he really is an artist—his trailer is full of paintings—and he's staying out here because it's cheap."

"And second?" Joe asked.

"I don't think he's one of the cactus thieves," Frank said. "I got him to talk about his involvement with Kidwell. It turns out that he has known Kidwell for a while. When he realized we considered Kidwell a suspect, Perez told him about it. They decided to try to get Grish off Kidwell's back by pointing the evidence toward Professor Townsend."

At that, Diane let out a gasp. "Why?" she asked.

"Because you and your father have been here long enough to look like suspects," Frank said.

"Perez is the one who planted that piece of organ pipe cactus under your truck. And get this: Perez also built that little trail marker near where your truck was parked. He was surprised that we took it seriously enough to spend a night up in the mountains."

"But he didn't cut the fuel line?" Joe asked. "And he didn't sabotage the climbing rope? What about Kidwell's truck and tools? The thieves are driving his truck, and we found his shovel in the trailer with the stolen cacti. I think if Kidwell's involved, so is Perez."

All of a sudden Perez stepped out from behind the motor home. "Pardon me for eavesdropping again, guys," he said. "I heard you talking about me as I came up, so I stopped to listen. The answer to whether David Kidwell is one of the cactus thieves is no. I'm sure he's not. I think he's being framed."

"Who's framing him?" Frank asked.

"I'm not sure," Perez said.

"Wait. Could it be Grish?" Frank said. "He's the one who suggested Kidwell might be a suspect."

"Grish? That's impossible," Joe said. "He's investigating this case. And he's a friend of Dad's. . . ." Joe paused while he thought about Frank's suggestion. "We did see him in his office talking to that cowboy Slim," he admitted.

"Grish could have sent the men in the yellow van to cut our fuel line," Frank said. Joe nodded. "He knew where we'd be. Now that I think of it, he even handled our climbing ropes before we used them last night."

"Yeah, and he always wanted to be at the center of everything," Joe said. "He wanted to know about any clue we found. Plus he was really serious about keeping this case under wraps."

"Oh, my gosh!" Diane exclaimed. "If Grish is involved, my father may be talking to him right now!"

"She's right," Joe said. "We'd better get over to the office quick!"

Frank and Joe jumped in the front seat of the car as Diane and Perez scrambled into the back. Joe spun the tires in the gravel as he sped away toward the office.

"I hope Dad's all right," Diane said. "Sometimes he can get too indignant for his own good."

"And if Grish is involved," Frank said grimly, "he may be dangerous. He tried to hurt us several times."

As they pulled into the office parking lot, they saw Grish, who appeared to be running from the direction of the pay phone. He didn't look up as they arrived but dashed to his official vehicle and drove off, leaving a cloud of dust.

"I don't like this," Joe said.

"Me either," Diane agreed, with an edge to her voice. "Where's my father?"

Diane jumped out of the car before Joe had even put it in park, and ran in the direction of the pay phone, around the corner of the building. Just as Joe turned the ignition off, he heard her scream.

Frank and Joe bolted out of the car and around the building. There they found Diane, bent over her father. He lay facedown under the pay phone, the back of his head bathed in blood.

14 The Body by the Road

"Don't move him," Diane said as they came up behind her. She was feeling her father's neck for a pulse. After a moment she said, "It's weak, but at least he's alive."

"Grish must have hit him," Frank said.

"He probably overheard the professor talking on the phone," Joe said.

"Could be," Frank said. "But one thing's for sure—Dad's in trouble. We have to figure out where Grish went, and fast."

Diane looked up. "We'd better call the police right now," she said. Then she added, "I can do that while you guys go after Grish."

"Right," Joe said. He touched her shoulder and said, "Good luck."

Frank grabbed Perez's arm. "Perez," he said, "I

want you to stay here with Diane. Grish might come back."

Perez looked at the professor and then said, "Okay, but you guys will need some help."

"Don't worry, we can handle it," Joe said.

"Make sure you tell the cops exactly what's going on," Frank said to Diane. "Maybe they can get hold of somebody at the state agriculture department. Definitely make it clear, though, that these thieves are dangerous. We've got the CB walkie-talkie in the car. If we can, we'll keep you posted."

Joe was already revving the engine impatiently when Frank jumped into the car.

"So where are we going, anyway?" Frank said as they sped away.

"I don't know," Joe said. "Grish probably has too much of a head start for us to catch up with him. But it's almost dark. Maybe we can spot his lights off to the side if he takes an alternate road."

Frank said, "Maybe he'll head back to town. Didn't you say there were a couple of vehicles left at the motel?"

Joe nodded. "That's true," he said. "The yellow van was still there when we left, and so was Kidwell's pickup truck. It's a long shot, but maybe we should head for the motel if we don't spot Grish along the way."

"It's possible the thieves were supposed to get together back at the motel," Frank said. "If they were smart, they'd be miles from here by now."

"Yeah," Joe said, "but don't forget that the two

guys in the trucks don't know we're on their trail. They probably think they're only pulling off one more job tonight, as the boss told them."

"Grish, the boss," Frank said. "Who'd have thought it? He seemed so dedicated to preserving the desert. I wonder what pushed him into doing this."

"Maybe it was money," Joe said. "He told us those big cacti are worth a lot."

"I have a feeling it's more than money," Frank said. "He's willing to hurt somebody."

"I don't care how angry he is," Joe said. "If he hurts Dad, he'll have more trouble on his hands than he knows what to do with."

Frank nodded. "That's the truth," he said quietly. "If he's smart, he'll just keep on going and forget about tonight's job."

"Yeah," Joe said. "But I have a feeling he's not that smart."

"That's what I'm afraid of," Frank said.

Joe pushed the car to its limit as they rode in silence, trying not to think about what could happen to their father if they didn't find him soon.

As they passed the motel in town, they saw the yellow van parked where it had been earlier. Beside it was Kidwell's truck.

"There!" Frank said, pointing. "On the other side of the parking lot. See it? Grish's truck. He's here."

Joe continued driving for another block and then parked as they devised a plan.

"No sign of the big trucks, though," Frank said. "I wonder what that means."

"I don't know," Joe said. "Maybe they came back here after I saw them leave, and then left again. They could already be out in Organ Pipe somewhere, getting ready to pull another job."

"They could be anywhere," Frank said. "Let's catch up with Grish first."

Joe turned around and drove back, parking around the corner from the motel so they could reconnoiter. As they approached Grish's truck, the door to one of the bungalows was flung open. A man, hidden by the long, obviously heavy bundle he was carrying over his shoulder, shuffled out toward the open side door of the yellow van. The bundle could have been a rolled-up carpet or a small cactus. More likely, though, it could have been a body wrapped in a blanket.

With a shout, the boys bolted toward the man, who hefted the bundle into the van and stepped in after it. He pulled the door shut behind him. Before the boys could reach him, he started the engine and backed the van straight toward them. As they dodged to keep from getting run over, he sped past them, swerved around, and then tore away down the street. When he swerved, they saw that Grish was driving.

"C'mon, Frank," Joe called as they ran to their car. They jumped in and raced after the van. "That might have been Dad he was loading in there," Joe

133

said. "How can we make him stop without getting Dad hurt?"

"I don't know," Frank said. "Wait, look! He's pulling over. This is way too easy. Something must be wrong."

The van swerved to the side of the road, and as they came up behind it, the bundle was tossed out the side and the van sped away.

Joe slammed on the brakes, then pulled off the road. Frank jumped out and ran to the bundle. "Dad?" he called. "Dad, are you in there? Are you okay? Oh, man, I hope you're okay."

Leaving the engine running, Joe jumped out to join his brother. "Be careful, Frank," he said. "Dad, can you hear me? Dad?"

There was no answer. The van was disappearing in the distance.

"Take a corner of the carpet," Frank said. "We'll open it slowly so we don't hurt him."

Together they peeled back the carpet, turning it slowly and unrolling it. Finally they unwrapped enough to see there was a person inside, with his mouth, wrists, and ankles taped.

But it wasn't Fenton. It was David Kidwell.

15 Making a Run for It

Frank removed the tape from Kidwell's mouth while Joe cut the tape from his wrists and ankles with his pocketknife. Kidwell seemed to have been drugged. He could hardly move and could only mumble unintelligibly.

"Let's get him in the car," Frank said. They lifted Kidwell and deposited him in the backseat. As Joe got the car on the road again, speeding after the van, Frank leaned over the back of the passenger seat and tried to talk to Kidwell.

"David, where were they taking you?" he asked.

Kidwell's mumbling was louder now as he made an effort to speak, but he was still incoherent.

"It's okay, David," Frank said. "We'll get you to a doctor soon."

Kidwell groaned and tried to sit up.

"David," Frank said, "Grish and those other guys have our father somewhere. We're trying to catch up, but we've lost them. Do you know where they were taking you?"

Kidwell became quiet, then finally muttered a word.

"What was that?" he asked. "I couldn't understand you."

Kidwell opened his mouth and slowly repeated the word. "A-la-mo," he said.

"Alamo?" Frank asked him. "Is that what you said? Is that the name of a place?"

"A-la-mo," Kidwell repeated, waving his hand as if to point.

Joe said, "Maybe there's a place on the map called Alamo. Grab the map, Frank."

Joe turned on the dome light as Frank unfolded the map.

"It could be anywhere," Frank said, scanning the topographic map. "Let's hope it's close by. Wait, here's something, not far from the highway through the park. Alamo Wash, it's called."

"Sounds like a Laundromat," Joe said.

"A wash is a dry riverbed," Frank said. "David, can you hear me? Is Alamo Wash what we're looking for?"

But Kidwell did not stir.

"They must have drugged him," Frank said. "Let's head for Alamo Wash and hope that's where they've taken Dad. Take the turnoff for the park. The wash crosses the highway about three or four miles inside. In the meantime I'm going to try the CB. If Perez is scanning, he can let the police know where we're going."

He took the walkie-talkie from beneath the seat. Switching it on, he said, "Break five. Break five. Perez, are you out there?" He paused to listen to the static hiss, hoping Perez would answer.

Joe said, "We were in such a hurry we didn't designate a channel."

"I know," Frank said. "But he's got that scanner in his trailer. It automatically switches from channel to channel until it comes to a signal." Pushing the transmit key, he tried again. "Break five. Break five. Perez, come back. Do you read, Perez? This is Frank. Over."

"Go, Frank," Perez's voice came back through the hiss. "Where are you?"

"We're on the highway," Frank told Perez. "We're headed to a place called Alamo Wash. It's about three or four miles inside the park. Did you get hold of the police? Over."

"Roger on that," Perez said. "Diane is waiting at the office with her dad. The police are sending a medevac helicopter. And the cops are on their way, too."

"Great," Frank said. "Tell them to find Alamo Wash. That's where Grish and his gang must have gone. We should be there in a few minutes. We've got David Kidwell with us. I think they drugged him. Over."

"Is he going to be all right?" Perez asked.

Frank glanced back over the seat. Under the dome light, Kidwell looked as if he was sleeping. "Maybe," Frank said. "You should tell the authorities we need medical help at Alamo Wash, too. Over."

"Roger," Perez said. "Good luck."

"Thanks," Frank said. "Out." He drew a long breath. "I hope we're headed to the right place," he said to Joe. "We probably won't get a second chance."

Joe did not answer as he stared ahead at the highway. Moments later they came to the turnoff that led south through Organ Pipe and on to the Mexican border. He slowed down and turned off the headlights when he passed the sign indicating the entrance to the park. In the moonlight, the road stretched out before them like a black ribbon through the dark desert.

"I think dousing the lights will make it easier to spot any lights off to the side," he said. "Keep your eyes open."

They both understood that Grish had the advantage. He probably knew every road, marked and unmarked, and every path and wash.

"What's that sign, Joe?" Frank asked.

Joe slowed to a stop, then backed up. Frank shone the flashlight on the sign, which read Alamo Wash. He swung the beam of light off to the left, where they could make out a dirt road turnoff.

"That's it," Joe said. "Let's pull up a little, so if they come out they won't spot the car." He drove a hundred yards forward, then pulled off the road and parked.

"Let's go," Frank said. "I'll take the flashlight and the CB. David, you stay here. . . . David?"

Kidwell didn't answer. The Hardys could only hope he'd be all right until help arrived. They had no choice but to leave him—their father's situation was urgent. Frank and Joe walked cautiously along the road for about a quarter of a mile, until they saw the glow of lights behind a hill up ahead.

"We found them!" Joe whispered.

"Yes," Frank whispered back. "Let's get off the road and head for that hill." They started off across the desert, moving carefully because the moon was not yet up and they didn't want to stumble through any cacti. They climbed the hill and looked down on the scene they had hoped to find. Below them, the headlights of the flatbed truck spotlighted an organ pipe cactus. Slim and the man in the plaid shirt were feverishly digging around the base of it. Frank could hear the sound of the flatbed truck engine, but even more clearly he could hear the diesel idling of the semi.

On the ground next to the cactus were some boards, probably to be used to frame the cactus once it was dug up. Grish walked into the light and seemed to be giving orders. He pointed at the base of the cactus.

The boys saw no sign of their father. They began a slow, careful descent of the hill, moving toward the thieves, trying to avoid slipping on the gravelly desert soil. They made their way around to the far side of the semi, where they saw the yellow van.

Shielded by the trailer from the men working on the cactus, the Hardys moved in closer. Joe could see that Grish, still standing in the light near the cactus, was wearing a pistol strapped to his hip. But more important, a dark shape caught Joe's eye near the back tires of the trailer. It had to be his father. He was tied up and had tape over his mouth. Joe nudged Frank and pointed.

Frank and Joe backed up and ducked behind a bush.

"You know what we have to do," Frank said.

"I'll create the diversion," Joe said. "When they come after me, you grab Dad and get out of here."

"How will you get away?" Frank asked.

"Same as you. They can't follow us in the dark unless they have heavy-duty flashlights. I'm guessing their minds are on digging and not on searching, so it will take them a minute to get to their flashlights. Maybe we'll get lucky and they'll forget all about chasing us and make a run for it."

"I hope you're right," Frank said.

They split up, with Joe moving around the perimeter of light and Frank edging in closer to the semi. Minutes passed as Frank waited. Then he heard a shout and saw the cowboy pointing into the darkness. Over the noise of the running engines, Frank couldn't hear what kind of disturbance Joe was making, but he could see that it was effective.

Pulling out his pocketknife, he ran to his father

140

and hastily cut the tape binding Fenton's wrists and ankles. Then he murmured, "Sorry, Dad," and ripped the tape from Fenton's mouth. "Can you run?" he asked.

"Yeah," Fenton muttered. "But my legs are stiff, so stay with me."

Linking hands to keep from getting separated in the dark, they trotted away from the semi, avoiding the trees and bushes. They slid down the embankment into the silt of a dry arroyo.

As they hit the soft sand, Frank heard the crack of a gunshot, and a bullet whistled over their heads.

16 A Long Desert Night

Frank and Fenton ducked under a bush just as a flashlight beam appeared at the top of the embankment and shone directly on them. They heard Grish say, "I suppose you think I'm as dumb as those two yahoos back there. Well, I'm not. And if you're not either, I suggest the two of you climb back up here just as quick as you can."

"Let's do it," Fenton muttered to Frank. "I don't think he wants to shoot anybody, but let's not give him a reason."

"I have five bullets left, Fenton," Grish said, "and you're not really up to a sprint, are you, old friend?"

Frank helped Fenton climb the embankment, and Grish motioned them back to the semi.

"Keep an eye on them," Grish said to the two

other men, who had given up chasing Joe in the darkness. "Where's your brother, Frank?"

"Don't worry," Frank said. "He's out there somewhere, waiting for you to make a wrong move."

Grish hesitated, waving his gun vaguely toward the darkness. "Well, just let him try something. Now you know what happens to people out here who butt into other people's business."

"What business is that, Grish?" Frank asked. "Stealing federal property? Making a bundle off something that belongs to everyone? Or just kidnapping and drugging innocent people and attempting murder?"

"What do you know?" Grish growled. "Do you know how long I've been stuck out here in this job? Do you know how many years I've put in? And now they're talking about downsizing the Forest Service, so I'll wind up with half as big a pension as I would have had. And I can't even collect that amount until ten years from now. What am I supposed to do in the meantime? Work in a fast-food restaurant? By selling these plants, I'm only getting what should have been mine in the first place."

"You'll get what you deserve!" Frank exclaimed. "The police are on their way. You can't go anyplace but Mexico from here."

"Mexico's just fine with me," Grish said. "We're half an hour from the border. And since things are a lot cheaper in Mexico, I can live a long time there on what I've made on these cactus plants."

"The police will be watching the highways for your trucks," Fenton said. "You'll never be able to sell these plants."

"No problem," Grish said. "If they catch up to us, we'll just forget about this load. We've already sold seven truckloads of cacti over the last couple of months. And by the way, the authorities know nothing about any of this. I haven't reported any of the missing cacti. And the only reason I let you boys in on the case was so I could keep track of your every move."

"Well, the authorities know now, old friend," Frank replied. "The cops are looking for you for injuring Professor Townsend. And when they catch up to you for that, you'll have to pay for kidnapping David Kidwell, too."

"Kidwell," Grish said with derision. "Now, there's a piece of work. If you hadn't interfered, he'd have gotten the blame for this whole thing."

A peculiar deep beating sound filled the air, over the noise of the diesel engine.

"Chopper!" Grish exclaimed. "Quick, turn those lights off!"

The blinking lights of the helicopter filled the sky. Slim ran to the flatbed and turned out its lights.

Just when Frank began to think he'd have a chance of getting away from Grish, a rough hand grabbed his collar. Then Frank felt the cold steel of the pistol against his cheek.

"Let's go," Grish said roughly. "Fenton, stand up. If you don't, I'll put a big hole in your nosy kid's head."

Holding Frank firmly by the collar, Grish herded the Hardys toward the van. "You guys are on your own!" he shouted to the other two men. "Leave all this stuff behind. You know where to meet. Be there!" With that, he slid open the van door and shoved Frank inside. "On the floor," he ordered Frank. "If I see your head pop up, you'll be sorry. Fenton, you get in front."

Without switching on the lights, Grish turned the van around and drove toward the highway just before the helicopter arrived above the trucks and shone a searchlight on the scene.

"That's good," Grish said as if to the pilot in the helicopter, his eyes on the searchlight in his rear-view mirror. "You keep looking back there at the trucks. Meanwhile, the Hardys and I will head for Mexico. No funny stuff, now, Fenton. I don't plan to hurt you. If you keep quiet when we get to the border, I'll release you in Sonoita. That's a little town just south of the border. You'll have no problem getting back across. But I mean it when I say no funny stuff. You Hardys have given me more than enough trouble. This last cactus would have brought another six thousand dollars."

"You could have gotten away before anybody figured out what you were up to," Fenton said. "Why go to the trouble of framing Kidwell?"

Grish scarcely slowed down as he swerved from

the dirt road onto the highway, his headlights still off. "Insurance," Grish said, "in case something went wrong, which it did when you Hardys showed up. Kidwell was a ready-made scapegoat who just happened to fall into my lap. No one could miss the connection between what was going on here and what happened to his company in Phoenix. That's why I rehired him after he slugged me. Actually, I hinted that I thought he might be involved in the thefts. That's why he took a swing at me."

Seconds after they passed the Hardys' car, parked on the side of the road, a pair of bright headlights came on dead ahead. Temporarily blinded, Grish shouted as he hit the brakes and the van skidded off the road and rolled onto its side.

Frank and Fenton rolled with the van as it slid. Both were unhurt. Concerned for Frank, Fenton climbed into the back, grabbed his arm, and pulled him up to a sitting position.

Grish kicked open the door and leaped out. "Get out of the van, and don't try anything," he yelled. "I still have my gun."

Grish turned to see who had caused the accident. Perez's pickup truck was parked in the middle of the road. Beside it, Perez held up his hands. "D-don't shoot!" he sputtered.

"Get over here with them," Grish shouted. "Now."

Perez walked over to Fenton and Frank, and all three raised their hands.

Grish glanced over at the pickup. "Give me the

keys," he said to Perez, who reached out and handed them over.

"Your truck should get me past the border," Grish said. "Don't anyone move." He took several steps backward, watching them, and then turned to run for the truck.

When Grish was about three feet from the truck, something flew through the air and knocked him flat. Frank couldn't believe it when he saw it was Joe, who had jumped off the top of the truck. On his back, Grish struggled to break free from Joe's hold, but Joe released him just long enough to land a solid punch on the man's jaw.

Next Fenton stepped over, grabbed Grish's pistol, and pointed it at him.

"Nice timing," Fenton said to Joe.

"Thanks," Joe said, releasing Grish now that his father had him covered. Joe stood up, and then bent over with his hands on his knees, trying to catch his breath. "I didn't think . . ." he gasped, "that I was . . . gonna to make it to you in time. As soon . . . as I saw Grish had you, I headed for the car, which we'd left by the side of the road. I was waiting in it when you drove by."

"Holy cow!" Perez exclaimed. "That was great, Joe! I knew the first time I met you guys that something great was going to happen. Man, this is just like the movies."

"Except that here, real people have gotten hurt," Frank said, his eyes on Grish. "How is Professor Townsend, Perez?"

"I think he's gonna be okay," Perez said. "Diane and I broke open the door to the office and moved him in there, where it was warm. The medevac helicopter arrived from Ajo just as I was leaving. I wanted to help you guys. When I saw your car parked here, I stopped to wait for you to come back. Then, when the helicopter showed up, and I heard the van tearing for the highway with its lights off, I figured Grish was headed this way. So I pulled my truck into the road and got set to hit him with my brights. I figured that might buy someone a chance to jump the driver. Smart move, huh?"

"Yeah, Perez," Joe said. "You almost got them killed in a car accident. Good thing you caught them right after the turn onto the highway, though, before he got up to highway speed."

"Exactly," Perez said enthusiastically. Joe wondered if Perez had done that purposely, and decided to give him the benefit of the doubt. He had to admit Perez's move had saved the day.

They heard footsteps and turned to find Kidwell stumbling into the light. Perez helped him sit down on the ground.

"I'm doing better," Kidwell said. "At least I think I am. I'm still groggy."

Fenton asked, "What did you give him, Grish?"

"Nothing that would hurt him," Grish said. "Sleeping pills. I was going to give him another dose about now, to keep him out until morning. After we dug up the cactus, my partners were set to go back to get Kidwell's pickup and clean up the

148

motel room. We were going to tip off the cops and go our separate ways. The cops would find Kidwell in his truck in the morning, right at the scene of the crime. All the evidence would point to him. He'd be blamed for the rattlesnake, the rappelling rope, and the fuel line as well as the cactus thefts. And of course he couldn't point to his accomplices, because he wouldn't know who they were. So the cops would figure he was uncooperative and they'd throw the book at him. Long prison term, end of story."

"What did I ever do to you, boss?" Kidwell asked Grish.

"Nothing," Grish replied. "Doesn't matter."

"Grish sent me into town earlier today," Kidwell said. "He said I had to pick up something at the motel. He said the guys there would give me what he wanted. They did, all right. They jumped me."

"And the shovel?" Joe asked. "What was so important about the shovel?"

"You probably don't know this," Kidwell explained, "but I had a great little landscape business in Phoenix."

"Grish told us a bit about it," Frank said.

"Well," Kidwell went on, "after I got cleared and paid off my lawyers, all I had left of my business was that silly shovel, which once belonged to my father. He was a landscaper, too, and he'd had his name engraved on it—same name as mine. It was the only thing I had to start over with. That's why it was so important to me."

From the direction of town, they saw one, then two, then three police cars come over the rise, lights flashing. Two of them slowed and turned off toward where the helicopter hovered with its searchlight beaming. The third continued straight and came to a stop in front of Perez's truck.

As two officers stepped from the vehicle, Fenton offered them his wallet to identify himself.

"So you're the one who was kidnapped?" one of the officers asked.

"Not exactly," Fenton said. "This man over here—David Kidwell—was kidnapped. I was just in the wrong place at the wrong time. And you'll want to take this man here—Winton Grisham—into custody for robbery, kidnapping, assault, you name it."

"I can see this is going to be a long night," the officer said as his partner snapped handcuffs on Grish and led him toward the patrol car, all the while reading him his rights. "We got a call from a young woman who gave us a pretty complicated picture of what's going on," the officer continued. "It was a good thing we got the highway patrol chopper involved. Why is the chopper over there, and you fellas all over here?"

"Two of the bad guys are over there," Perez said. "And the biggest bad guy, the one in the patrol car, was making a run for the border. Just like in the movies."

"So you stopped him?" the officer asked.

"No, sir," Perez said. He pointed at Joe, and said,

"It was him. Joe came out of nowhere and cut him off at the pass! Like in the old westerns!"

"Not exactly," Frank said. "In the old westerns, the bad guys would have been stealing cattle, not plants. And they'd have been on horseback, not in trucks. And there's no way they'd have been caught by a helicopter. And then there are details like the walkie-talkies and the power winch for lifting the plants."

"Yeah," Joe said. "Except for that stuff, it was exactly like the Old West."

R·L·STINE'S
GHOSTS OF FEAR STREET ®

1 HIDE AND SHRIEK 52941-2/$3.99
2 WHO'S BEEN SLEEPING IN MY GRAVE? 52942-0/$3.99
3 THE ATTACK OF THE AQUA APES 52943-9/$3.99
4 NIGHTMARE IN 3-D 52944-7/$3.99
5 STAY AWAY FROM THE TREE HOUSE 52945-5/$3.99
6 EYE OF THE FORTUNETELLER 52946-3/$3.99
7 FRIGHT KNIGHT 52947-1/$3.99
8 THE OOZE 52948-X/$3.99
9 REVENGE OF THE SHADOW PEOPLE 52949-8/$3.99
10 THE BUGMAN LIVES! 52950-1/$3.99
11 THE BOY WHO ATE FEAR STREET 00183-3/$3.99
12 NIGHT OF THE WERECAT 00184-1/$3.99
13 HOW TO BE A VAMPIRE 00185-X/$3.99
14 BODY SWITCHERS FROM OUTER SPACE 00186-8/$3.99
15 FRIGHT CHRISTMAS 00187-6/$3.99

 Available from Minstrel® Books
Published by Pocket Books

THE WHITE HOUSE IS FULL OF SECRETS!

Molly Wright solves mysteries in the White House with the help of some ghostly friends.

Money Madness

Nest Egg Nightmare
(Coming in mid-December 1996)

Dolley's Detectives
(Coming in mid-February 1997)

By Gibbs Davis

A MINSTREL® BOOK

Published by Pocket Books

1263